Has Terence O'Shea fallen in love with the wrong roommate?

"A right good farm wife she'll make some lucky man." Terry O'Shea's smiling face radiated affection.

Lindsey's heart dropped to the soles of her feet.

Patti laughed joyously. "Talk about blarney. Terence, take my suitcase to my temporary abode." She looked around the charming green apartment. "I can't wait to get back."

Terry's merry whistle and excellent spirits depressed Lindsey even more. Try as she would, she just couldn't be glad for Patti.

The smaller nurse flopped into a chair. "Good to be home, even though the farm is wonderful. I could fall in love with Shane O'Shea if I were older or he were younger."

"There's always his son." Lindsey managed to say.

COLLEEN L. REECE is one of the most popular authors of inspriational romance. With over ninety books in print, including nineteen **Heartsong Presents** titles, Colleen's army of fans continues to grow. Colleen resides in Washington state and has written under the pen name Connie Loraine for her previous books in the Shepherd of Love Hospital Series.

Books by Colleen L. Reece

Books by Connie Loraine

Don't miss out on any of our super romances. Write to us at the following address for information on our newest releases and club information.

Heartsong Presents Readers' Service
P.O. Box 719
Uhrichsville, OH 44683

A Kindled Spark

Colleen L. Reece

Shepherd of Love Hospital Series

Heartsong Presents

A note from the author:
I love to hear from my readers! Write to me at the following address:

Colleen L. Reece
Author Relations
P.O. Box 719
Uhrichsville, OH 44683

ISBN 1-55748-922-X

A KINDLED SPARK

© 1996 by Colleen L. Reece. All rights reserved. Except for use in any review, the reproduction or utilization of this work in whole or in part in any form by any electronic, mechanical, or other means, now known or hereafter invented, is forbidden without the permission of the publisher, Heartsong Presents, P.O. Box 719, Uhrichsville, Ohio 44683.

All of the characters and events in this book are fictitious. Any resemblance to actual persons, living or dead, or to actual events is purely coincidental.

Cover illustration by Gary Maria.

PRINTED IN THE U.S.A.

one

Thy word is a lamp unto my feet, and a light unto my path.
(Psalm 119:105)

Redheaded Lindsey Best, surgical nurse, slumped against the muraled wall outside the Shepherd of Love hospital director's office. Lindsey stared at the inscription engraved on the always-open door, but for the first time since she had come to the hospital to complete her final training before graduation, she wasn't really seeing it. No trace of her usual smile lurked on her soft lips, and her eyes had no sparkle. Even the freckles on her tip-tilted nose, the ones Lindsey's parents stoutly insisted were fairy dust, looked drab and dull.

"Why so pensive?" a laughing voice demanded.

"Oh, to live in a world of your own, far away from mundane hospital life," a second voice caroled.

Lindsey straightened her lanky body, crossed her arms over her pale-green uniform, and looked down at her tormentors. Tiny Japanese Shina—pronounced *Sheena*—Ito capably cared for mothers and babies in Obstetrics, and the mothers adored her. Blonde, blue-eyed Patti Thompson stood four inches shorter than Lindsey; her deceptive fragility hid the endurance necessary to deal with the multitudes who swarmed to Outpatient.

A reluctant smile tugged at Lindsey's lips. "Have you no respect for your elders?"

Patti clutched Shina in mock fear. "Behold the wise one. Even though we're all twenty-four, we are required to bow before my roommate's extra month of life on this terrestrial ball."

"You should. It's time your showed deference to your betters."

Irrepressible Patti raised her eyebrows. Innocence crept into her face. "Since when is older better?" Before Lindsey could reply, Patti and Shina chorused in unison, "We know. You're not better, you're the Best." Patti added, "You've told us enough times."

Shina's trill of laughter brought a grin that chased away the last of their friend's reflective mood. "So what are you two doing lurking outside the director's office at this time of day?"

"That's gratitude for you. We came to get you for supper." Patti raised a haughty chin.

"And to see if you learned anything more about who will take the director's place while he is on sick leave," Shina added honestly. A little frown marred her smooth forehead and she looked affectionately at the murals of sea, forest, and mountain scenes that transformed corridor walls to restful beauty. "I can't imagine having someone new in charge."

"Neither can I." Patti turned serious. Her wide blue eyes darkened. "He's been here ever since the hospital opened. Why, he's as much a part of it as Nicholas Fairchild." Her walk lost some of its spring. "Lindsey, did you learn anything?"

"Just that several persons are under consideration." She matched her longer steps to those of her friends. "The problem is two-fold: first, finding a dedicated Christian who will uphold the standards of the hospital itself—second, someone who is a top administrator." Her heart warmed, remembering how wealthy Mr. Fairchild had carried out his vision of a hospital where medical and surgical skills went hand in hand with prayer, and served rich and poor alike. Shepherd of Love never turned a patient away for lack of funds, even when the patient needed long-term care. Neither did the hospital have fund drives or ask for money. Needs were presented to God—and they were met by those who were impressed by God to support the hospital's unique goals.

In the years since it opened, Shepherd of Love had worked closely with the other excellent Seattle hospitals, winning their respect and admiration. In turn, the hospital on the hill faithfully transferred patients to Harborview, Swedish, Children's, or whatever other facility offered more specialized care when it was needed.

"An acting director won't be the only new face around here," Patti observed. She hugged her arms across her chest.

"Really? Who's leaving?" Shina stopped and stared at her.

"The chaplain is going to retire." Patti blinked hard. "He said he would stay until we found a new man—or woman—but since his wife has grown frail, he needs to spend more time with her. Specialists feel confident she can regain her strength by wintering in the southwest where it's warmer." The blonde nurse sighed. "Why do things always have to change? Who would I go to if I ever had a problem?"

"Which you don't," Lindsey teased. "Except changing *Patty* to *Patti*."

"It's classier—and I might have a problem sometime." Patti sniffed. "Anyway, it would be a lot easier to talk with our very own chaplain than having to spill out to a stranger."

"He—or she—won't be a stranger long at Shepherd of Love," Shina softly put in. Her dark eyes glowed and she flung her arms wide in an unaccustomed show of exuberance. "Look at us when we came. Three scared rabbits—"

"Not me," Patti interrupted.

"Not I," Lindsey corrected. Her eyes shone with fun and her voice rose to a treble pitch. " 'P-p-please, nurse,' " she mimicked. " 'I—I've lost Outpatient.' "

Patti groaned. "I'll never live that one down! Of course, I remember things, too. Like a certain sleepy nurse after a long, hard night in Surgery who mistook hair dressing for toothpaste."

Lindsey made a horrible face. "Yecch. I can still taste that awful stuff." When Shina laughed, Lindsey scowled and twirled an imaginary mustache. "Why jeerest thou?

Methinks small maiden has soon forgotten the solemn presentation of a step stool at our first Christmas here as full-fledged nurses."

"*Me* thinks if we don't get showered and to the dining room they'll be out of food," Shina reminded, refusing to dignify Lindsey's taunt by recognizing it.

When Shepherd of Love Hospital was built, one of the things Nicholas Fairchild had insisted on was cozy, attractive decor. As much as possible, the creamy white building, perched on its wooded Seattle hill, was designed to be homelike. A covered, connecting passage led to the staff residence hall—women downstairs, men up. Built in the form of a T, the crossbar offered library, living room, laundry facilities, and game room. The three nurses lived at the far end of the long corridor. For some time after coming to work at the hospital, Shina had remained with her parents, who held traditional views about her living at home until she married. Finally, concern over Shina commuting, especially in winter, overcame her father's reservations and she moved into the charming yellow apartment near her friends.

The mini-suites—tastefully decorated living rooms, bedrooms, kitchenettes, and baths—offered views of either mountain or Puget Sound. Patti and Lindsey's double was done in soft greens. The door to a nearby rose suite stood open. At the extreme end, a cream and blue apartment also invited passersby.

"This end of the corridor feels deserted since Jonica and Nancy married," Patti complained. "I'm almost tempted to move into one of their old rooms."

"What? You'd leave me?" Why should the jesting words stir a nameless fear in Lindsey's heart?

Patti spun from her contemplation of the two empty suites. Mischief danced in her eyes and she cocked her head to one side. "One never can tell," she said mysteriously. The next minute a rush of warmth chased away her teasing. "Of course I'm not going to leave you, even though you boss me."

"Not boss. Just train in the way you should go." Lindsey ducked her roommate's pretend blow and headed into their apartment. "Want first shower?"

"Please. It takes me longer to dress."

"True." Lindsey snatched a simple cream skirt and blouse outfit from the closet and laid it on the bed. "That's because you have more clothes and can't decide which outfit will make you most fetching in the eyes of the interns."

"Fetching! You sound like a book." The rush of the shower drowned out the rest of Patti's good-natured grumble.

Thirty minutes later the three hungry nurses entered the cool, green-painted staff dining room with its spotless white curtains swaying in the breeze from open, screened windows. Tables for eight offered distance enough between to allow individual discussions. Food was served buffet style instead of cafeteria. Fresh flowers and candles on the tables gave the room the atmosphere of a fine restaurant.

The nurses arrived late enough so only a few staff members still idled over after-dinner coffee, yet contrary to Shina's earlier dour prediction, no food shortage existed. Patti complained, "I don't know why I keep eating here. One of these days I'll be this round." She reached for an iced butter ball and another hot roll.

"Which?" Lindsey teased.

Patti shrugged and ignored her. The next moment the blue eyes that matched her soft cotton dress widened. "My goodness, would you look at that?"

Shina, glowing like a peony in her pink blouse and matching printed skirt, glanced over her shoulder. "Who is he?"

"Who is who?" Used to Patti's making much of the ordinary, Lindsey finished cutting her meat before looking up. All three nurses had the chance to date as often as they wished, but Patti had a new rave on the average of once a month, so Lindsey took Patti's present excitement with a grain of salt.

Lindsey raised her head and looked past Shina. A shock

wave ran down her spine. A tall stranger, handsome enough to be a movie star, stood just inside the dining room doorway. Thirtyish, straight as a javelin, he stared across at the nurses' table, an unreadable expression on his lean face.

"You don't suppose—" Shina began, but Patti interrupted her.

"Have you ever seen a handsomer man?"

"Not since Rhett Butler," Lindsey admitted, unable to tear her gaze from the newcomer even when she saw amusement in his midnight-black eyes.

"Just remember, I saw him first," Patti whispered. "Oh, dear, he's leaving!"

The dismay in her voice made Shina giggle. "He might be a doctor."

"Probably a patient's husband," Lindsey callously told Patti and went back to her dinner as if the brief interlude had not left her strangely shaken.

"Just my luck. The most spectacular man who's come to Shepherd of Love since I've been here and—" she paused. Hope sprang into her face. "Maybe he's our replacement chaplain."

Lindsey shook her head until the shining fall of red hair bounced. "Too good-looking."

"What does that have to do with it?" Patti challenged. "Is there a law or commandment that chaplains have to be old as Methuselah?"

"No, just wiser than Solomon." Shina's white teeth flashed in a grin.

"Mark my words, that man is no chaplain!" The vehemence of Lindsey's tone startled even her. Why had she said such a thing?

It didn't faze Patti, who doggedly asked, "How do you know, great oracle?" She leaned forward as if her life depended on the reply.

"I just do." Lindsey couldn't explain. Something about the stranger had set her pulse quick-stepping, even while faintly repelling her.

"After we finish dinner we could walk through the hospital," Patti suggested blandly. She bit into the roll that had cooled while she checked out the man in the doorway.

"Whatever for?" Shina's fork dropped with a tiny clatter. "I know you love this place, but didn't you just come off eight hours of duty?"

Lindsey snorted in the unladylike way that always brought a frown from her roomie. "Patricia Thompson, are you actually suggesting a man-hunting expedition in Shepherd of Love? How old are you, anyway, twenty-four or fourteen?"

Patti put on her best injured, you-don't-understand expression. "How can you accuse me of such a thing?" She loftily turned her head and looked out the window. "Besides, it's too late. He just climbed into a black sports car and drove off." She sighed. "Well, at least I won't have to run competition with you two."

Laughing and joking, they finished dinner, relaxed for a time on the shaven deep green lawn near the staff residence, and watched a spectacular sunset over Puget Sound. Soon the death of summer would drive them indoors. The thought depressed Lindsey.

What's the matter with me, she wondered. *Seasons never bother me. I love each in turn. All day I've been jittery and I have no idea why.*

"Oh-oh. Looks like a storm's brewing." Patti jumped up and headed toward the back entrance to the residence hall. Shina followed, but Lindsey lingered. She secretly loved storms: lightning that danced above the city; the sonic boom of thunder; even the torrents of rain that made Seattle the Emerald City. Yet she found herself shivering when an enormous inky cloud blew in from the west and parked directly over the hospital. Like a portent of doom it spread its wings and cast a black shadow that made the watching nurse shudder with excitement—and something more.

Transfixed by the awe-inspiring sight, Lindsey stood with clenched hands until the first enormous raindrop splatted against her upturned face. Another. Then a downpour. She barely reached shelter before the full force of the unexpected summer squall broke. Inside, she shook herself like a water spaniel, pressed her face to the shining-paned window, and watched the storm rage.

"I may be younger and in need of guidance but at least I know enough to get in out of the rain," Patti smugly remarked. Shina smiled at the by-play as familiar to her as the roommates.

Lindsey whirled from her observation point. "Do you ever have a feeling something is going to happen?"

"Like what?" Patti abandoned her teasing and began brushing her hair.

"I don't know." Lindsey bit her lip. She looked appealingly at Shina, but met a puzzled stare. She wanted to cry out her feeling that more than a storm cloud hovered over the hospital they loved. She could not. The fragility of what she could sense but not identify made it impossible.

"Lindsey?" Patti's voice came to her through the Turkish towel Lindsey had snatched up to dry her face.

"Yes?"

"Nothing. For a minute there you looked, I don't know—fey."

"Fey? Now who's using book language? Besides, I thought *fey* meant 'doomed.' " Her rich laugh pealed out.

For the first time, Patti didn't respond. "It also means 'visionary, otherworldly.' Sometimes it's uncanny how you sense things before they happen." She crossed her arms over her chest and shivered.

Lindsey dropped the towel in amazement. "This isn't like you, Patti." Her troubled gaze sought Shina but found no reassurance, just growing concern. "What do you think I am, a witch?"

"Don't be ridiculous!" She sounded more Patti-like. "It's

just that once in a while I wonder. Remember that time you were on swing shift and we went to church on your night off? In the middle of the service, you felt you should go to Surgery. Five minutes after you got there and into scrubs the ambulances started bringing people in from a bad accident."

"I remember, but what has that to do with being fey?"

"I just wonder if you've been given a special gift of insight." Patti rushed on, heedless of the exchange of glances between Lindsey and Shina. "Remember in Acts where Peter quoted the prophet Joel? God said in the last days He would pour out His Spirit; that their sons and daughters, His servants and handmaidens would prophesy."

"Many Christians believe these are the last days, but we can't be sure this prophecy has fully come to pass," Shina objected.

"Even if it has, I'm no prophet." Lindsey crossed to the window and peered out. "The storm is lifting and we'd best get some sleep. I go back on nights tomorrow."

Patti continued to look troubled. "I wish I knew what you think is going to happen."

"I do, too," Lindsey soberly said. "All we can do is pray about it."

"Then let's do it right now." An odd intensity filled Patti's quiet voice. The nurses knelt, hands clasped in a friendship circle. Each asked God's blessing on the hospital and all who served or came there. It wasn't the first time they had joined in prayer, yet Lindsey had a curious feeling about it. All the scoffing and telling herself she was getting too imaginative couldn't erase the memory of Patti's words.

Shina murmured good night and slipped away. Lindsey and Patti went to their separate bedrooms, but the cheerful red-headed nurse lay sleepless in spite of a tired body. She relived the fateful night when something beyond herself compelled her to rise and go where she was desperately needed. If she had remained in church until the service ended. . . She shut down on the thought. No one would ever know how much, if any, difference she had made, but Lindsey would never forget Dr. Paul Hamilton's fervent, "Thank God you are here!" when he found her there and ready.

Now she pondered. Neither he nor his wife Jonica, night charge nurse at the time, questioned then or later how Lindsey happened to be on hand. She had felt shy of mentioning her experience, except to Patti and Shina. She remembered their questions. Had she heard a voice? Was it a premonition? Lindsey had no answers. She rejected Patti's explanation. She didn't have an ounce of mysticism in her. And yet. . .

She fell asleep hoping the following day would dawn bright and beautiful. Gray days could give people the gloomies.

Lindsey received her wish. Every leaf and blade of grass shone from the recent shower. Sunlight sent gold motes dancing in the bay, along with tiny whitecaps from a gentle, but mischievous breeze. How good to be alive and young in God's beautiful world!

"I don't think I could ever be happy living where I couldn't see the mountains," she told her friends at breakfast.

"What if you marry someone who lives elsewhere?" Patti could be extremely practical when she chose. This morning she looked like a ripe peach in her pants uniform of the same color. Shina's pale-daffodil outfit made her more flowerlike than ever. Both enviously eyed Lindsey's jeans and plaid shirt, designed to withstand the assault of her multitude of brothers and sisters whenever she visited her family.

Glad for the day off, Lindsey grinned. "I'm hoping God has a nice man from right here in Seattle all picked out for me." Why should the handsome face of the stranger in the dining doorway flash into her mind? Nonsense! She quickly stood. "Bye, slaves."

"Don't rub it in," Patti retorted, then relented enough to wish her a good day.

Humming the first line of "This is My Father's World" half under her breath, Lindsey headed for the dining room exit in her usual long, ground-covering lope. Just inside the door she glanced over her shoulder to smirk at her friends. Shina's warning cry, "Watch out!" came too late.

The next instant Lindsey crashed to the floor, victim of a head-on collision with a man striding into the dining room at a pace even faster than her own.

two

In the dazed moment after the crash, Lindsey heard a rich voice say, "I certainly didn't expect to have anyone fall for me on my first visit to the hospital. You aren't hurt, are you, miss? Or is it nurse?"

The comment in an unfamiliar voice didn't even register. An awful thought attacked Lindsey. Was it—it couldn't be the striking stranger who had coolly surveyed the nurses, then drove away in a sports car! She felt hot blood swirl into her face before her overdeveloped sense of humor came to her rescue. Leave it to her. Patti might have seen the stranger first, but *she* had certainly made the first impression. Lindsey scrambled to her feet and looked up, fully expecting to meet the amused dark gaze that had stirred her at dinner the night before.

She gasped. Her mouth fell open. Had she struck her head when she fell? Midnight-black eyes and hair couldn't change to laughing gray-blue beneath wavy, polished mahogany hair, could they?

The wide-shouldered stranger, an inch or two taller than she, steadied Lindsey when she involuntarily stepped back. Laughter gave way to concern. "You are hurt. What a clumsy oaf I am, charging through doors as if pursued by howling banshees." He led her to the nearest table, pulled out a chair, and gently forced her to sit. "Would you like a glass of water?"

"No. You—I—it was someone else." Of all the inane remarks, that had to be the worst. A glimpse of Patty and Shina with hands over their mouths to cover their mirth didn't help one bit. "Perhaps I could use some water," Lindsey mumbled, more to get rid of him and give herself time to collect her wits than because she wanted a drink.

"Right." He strode away at the same breakneck pace he had just decried. Who was he, anyway? No one she'd ever seen before. Decidedly attractive in a rugged sort of way, unlike the taller movie star visitor of the night before, although she'd guess they were about the same age.

Penitence filled her caregiver's face when he returned with a brimming glass of ice water. "Forgive me for making light of your fall."

"It's all right. I shouldn't have been walking so fast." Her shaken nerves steadied. "I'm not hurt."

"Thanks be," he told her. The worry in his eyes fled. "You are—"

"Lindsey Best, surgical nurse." Patti and Shina had controlled themselves enough to come over and show belated concern, although Lindsey knew merriment still threatened to break through their deceptively calm exteriors. "This is Patti Thompson, Outpatient, and Shina Ito, Obstetrics."

Her rescuer stood. "It's a pleasure to meet you." He ducked his head in acknowledgment and his eyes glowed, bluer than before. "I'm Terence O'Shea, hoping to be the new chaplain here at your hospital."

The look of amazement on Patti's face repaid Lindsey, who wickedly said, "You aren't quite what we expected."

"No?" He raised questioning eyebrows.

"It's just that our former chaplain was much older," Lindsey hastened to explain when neither of her friends made an attempt to enter the conversation. Delighting in the chance to get even with them for laughing, she casually glanced at her watch, then at Shina and Patti. "I hate to break up this happy gathering, but do you know what time it is?"

"Mercy, we'll be late." Patti roused from her unusual silence and grabbed Shina's arm. "Nice meeting you." She dimpled. Shina murmured something similar, and they hurried out—but not before sending Lindsey a furtive glance that promised a reckoning later in the day.

"I must go, too," her companion told her. "Don't want to be late for my interview with the board. If it goes well, I'd like to tell you about it." He glanced at her shirt and jeans. "It looks like you're ready to go out and about."

"Yes. My family has a sprawling, old-timey house on Queen Anne Hill. I promised to spend the day with them. I go back on night duty this evening." She rose, in full control again, and impulsively held out her hand. "Good luck, Mr. O'Shea."

His strong hand engulfed hers. "It's Terence, and I thank you, Miss Best."

"Lindsey."

"A truly sturdy name," he approved. Twinkles danced in his eyes. He gave her a little bow that in anyone else would have seemed affected, but somehow it fit his personality and did nothing to detract from his manliness.

She watched him go out in the pell-mell manner she often tried to curb in herself. Although her heart and pulse remained steady, she felt warmed. "He has to have Irish ancestry," she told the now-empty room. "Wonder if he's as full of blarney as his name suggests?" Lindsey thought of the steady look in his strong face. "Patti or anyone else shouldn't have a problem taking troubles to him," she soliloquized. She remembered an expression her grandmother often used and smiled. Terence O'Shea really did warm the cockles of one's heart. *How do you know?* reason demanded. Lindsey just laughed. A face as honest as the new applicant's couldn't even conceal his feelings, let alone a deep, dark, indescribable past. So he thought she had a sturdy name. She would need time to decide if she liked that!

The excellent Metro King County bus service to Queen Anne Hill from the hospital meant Lindsey didn't need a car, a fact for which she was profoundly grateful. She didn't go around advertising the fact, but she turned over part of her salary to help five younger brothers and sisters. They in turn adored their older sister and studied hard to make her proud of them.

Lindsey's keen gaze softened. Her parents' neighborhood delicatessen took in more than enough for the family's needs, but Ramsey and Linda Best gave away enough food to feed a regiment. Not one of their children protested. They had been raised in an if-we-have-it-God-expects-us-to-share-it atmosphere. When they wanted something out of the ordinary, they mowed lawns or baby-sat. Each had contributed something toward putting Lindsey through nursing school.

She reached the conclusion that no one had a better family and the bus stop a block from her home at the same time. She swung down the step, loped up the sidewalk, and paused. The old house was inviting, from the deep yard, grass worn in spots by countless ball games, to the welcoming front porch with its rockers and swing. Spotless in a fresh coat of white paint put on by the family, it reminded Lindsey of a Victorian chaperone who spreads her skirts and settles down, refusing to budge.

She laughed at her fancy, raced up the steps and flung wide the screen door. "Mom? Dad?" One would be at the deli, along with a brother, sister, or two.

"In here."

Lindsey followed her nose and the sound of her mother's voice to a high-ceilinged kitchen, fragrant with the aroma of baking beans and yeasty rolls. A rocker sat conveniently nearby, occupied by an orange and white cat. Lindsey hugged the mother from whom she had inherited her looks, scooped up the cat, and dropped into the chair with her purring bundle. "Mmm. When's lunch?"

"Didn't you have breakfast?" her older edition asked.

"Hours ago. Well, one hour." Tension she didn't realize she'd carried melted like the butter Mom lavishly spread on a hot roll. She handed the roll to her daughter, and a second roll soon followed. "When I meet Mr. Right, if I do, I'll bring him here and show him you. It will clinch the deal."

Lindsey irrelevantly said.

"What a nice thing to say!" Her mother pinkened beneath the sprinkling of freckles on clear skin so like her daughter's. She cocked one eyebrow, pulled down the corners of her mouth, and looked smug, a trait Lindsey unconsciously copied without being aware of it. "Any new prospects?"

Lindsey stuck her long legs straight out before her. "Maybe. Well, sort of, only I don't know for sure." Her capable hand with its long fingers moved rhythmically over the cat's back. He rumbled his appreciation.

"Which translates to—?" Mischief shone in Linda Best's eyes, green-tinted from the green-and-white checked blouse she wore.

They were still talking when different shifts of the family arrived for lunch. Each new wave brought familiar banter and complaints that Lindsey didn't get home often enough. All thought of her day-before premonitions, if that's what they had been, dissolved. She decided to walk back to the deli with her father and visit between customers. The smell of good cheese and meats, a whiff of potpourri, the tang of onions and pickle, all brought back a thousand memories.

"I am so glad we live in Seattle," she told her father while lending a hand at making sandwiches.

"So am I. If that makes us provincial, who cares?" Her sandy-haired father brandished a slim spatula like a sword, then swiftly spread mayonnaise on a split French roll. "Someday when all the kids are grown, I want to take your mother traveling, but we'll always come back to the Pacific Northwest."

The afternoon sped by on runner's feet. Lindsey at last tore herself away. "Have to get back to the hospital and sleep a few hours." She gave her dad a hug and started toward the door with its merry, jingling bell that announced customers. "Don't work too hard."

"Or you." Blue eyes looked deep into hazel. "We're mighty

proud of you, Lindsey. Not just for what you do, but for who you are."

For some unexplainable reason, she wanted to put her head on her father's shoulder and cry. Instead, she blinked long, wet lashes and saluted. "Thanks." He came out on the porch he had added to the deli when he took it over, a big, gentle man in an apron that showed signs of his trade. Lindsey turned at the corner and waved. Something about him reminded her of Terence O'Shea.

In a heartbeat, she mentally left one world for her other. By the time she reached Shepherd of Love, Lindsey the daughter had submerged herself into Lindsey the nurse, anticipating a long night of serving others. She went straight to her apartment. Patti and Shina would be at supper, but they knew to expect her when they saw her. Lindsey closed her bedroom door, set her alarm, and fell into dreamless sleep. A little after ten she awakened. Long before her eleven o'clock shift began, Lindsey, acting night charge nurse pending the selection of a replacement for Jonica Carr Hamilton, stood checking the shining surgical instruments that must be ready and waiting when needed. She slipped away to attend the prayer service held at the beginning of each shift. Shepherd of Love employed only dedicated Christian personnel and one way they gave their best service was through mingled prayer for the patients they served in Christ's stead.

Her first four hours proved uneventful. No accident cases came in. No surgical emergencies. Lindsey used the time to diminish a mountain of paperwork. Her staff did routine duties they might not have time for later. At 3:00 A.M. she strode the silent halls to the dining room. Others on night shift throughout the hospital joined her, giving thanks for the quiet night.

They rejoiced too soon. The scream of an ambulance taunted them, and sent doctors and nurses flying back to their wards. A flurry of activity ensued. "Bus wreck," came the terse explanation from Emergency. "No fatalities. Abrasions and contusions, except for a gashed leg." The disembodied voice went on with vital statistics taken on the scene by well-qualified paramedics. Lindsey quickly briefed her staff, double-checked the instrument table, and stood at the doorway, ready to receive and reassure the pale-faced patient who weakly said he was okay.

"Will you call my wife, please, nurse? And my boss? I was on my way to work. I work in a bakery and start at four each morning. The boss will have to get backup for me."

"Of course." Lindsey made two quick calls before the hastily summoned junior surgeon arrived. She returned to say the patient's wife would be there by the time her husband was ready to be released. She laid expert fingers on the pulse in his wrist, noting how he visibly relaxed at the assurance.

The gash in the leg proved to be fairly deep, but not serious. The surgeon capably sutured and bandaged it, then ordered the patient to go home and stay off his feet for a time.

Distress filled the man's face. "I can't. We're barely making it on what I earn. If I lose my job, I don't know what I'll do." He raised up on one elbow.

The surgeon gently pushed him down. "It's only for a day or two. I'm sure your boss will understand."

"What if he doesn't?" the anxious man retorted.

Lindsey intervened. "When I called, your boss said to tell you to take what time you need," she told the patient. "He said you hadn't taken a vacation since you started working for him and you deserved a few days off. With pay," she added when the man's expression remained heavy.

"Thank God!"

"That's what this hospital is all about," the surgeon said quietly. "Nurse Best, I believe this man's wife is here. I'll sign the release form."

A few minutes later doctor and nurses watched the sprightly little woman trot alongside her husband's wheelchair, holding his hand and fussing over him. "One of the most rewarding parts of medicine," the surgeon commented. He yawned. "I guess that does it for this shift. Want a cup of coffee after we get cleaned up?"

"Thanks, but I need to make my report to the day shift," Lindsey said. She stifled a yawn of her own, marveling. She never felt tired while on duty, but once her shift ended, weariness set in. She threw aside her stained scrubs, promised herself a shower when she got to the apartment, and slid into the pants and knit shirt she kept on hand. Her stomach growled just as she finished reporting to the day charge nurse. "Right on schedule." Lindsey laughed. "Patty and Shina will be at breakfast by the time I get there."

Her fast, gliding walk carried her down corridors, stairs, and into the dining room. She selected creamy oatmeal, fresh strawberries, a blueberry muffin, and an enormous glass of orange juice from the buffet.

"No eggs or bacon this morning?" the friendly attendant who kept fresh food supplies coming to the buffet table inquired.

"This is enough to at least get me started," Lindsey told him. She threaded her way across the room to the last seat at Shina and Patti's table. "I'll help even the odds," she teased. "Five males and two females is a bit lopsided.

"I don't know about that." Patti coolly helped herself to a strawberry threatening to topple off Lindsey's plate. Her pale lavender uniform and Shina's pink made their friend feel rumpled and worn by comparison.

Lindsey dug in, making giant inroads on her breakfast and listening to the usual hospital scuttlebutt.

"I heard there was a spot of excitement last night," one of the interns offered.

"Really?" "Where?" "When?" Questions flew.

Lindsey continued eating.

"Personnel." He grinned maddeningly.

"What happened?"

"Prowler, I guess, but no one can figure out why. Papers thrown all over the place but, at least so far, nothing significant seems to be missing."

"Nothing significant?" Lindsey's quick mind seized on the word. She put down her fork and leaned toward him. "What *is* missing?"

He looked surprised and a bit abashed. "Sorry. Slip of the tongue. As far as I know, nothing at all." His forehead wrinkled. "Funny. You'd think if someone broke into a hospital it would be after drugs." He glanced at a clock on the wall near the door. "Hi-ho. It's off to work I'd better go or this intern will never achieve resident status. What I'd give for one full, uninterrupted night's sleep."

"Appreciate what you do get, Sleepy," hard-hearted Patti said. "Dopey here needs to go to bed, too." She pointed the comment toward a yawning Lindsey.

"If I weren't refusing to play your silly little game I could say a few things about a certain Grumpy," Lindsey squelched her. "See you." A chorus of laughter followed her out the door, this time unhindered by tall, dark strangers and mahogany-haired men hoping to be chaplains.

One shower and eight full hours of sleep later, Lindsey awakened to the sound of the outer apartment door opening. "Patti?"

"Shina. May I come in?" She sounded hesitant. Shina never intruded on anyone's privacy.

"Of course." Lindsey sat up in bed. "Where's Patti?"

"Man-hunting." Shina parked herself on the foot of Lindsey's bed and stretched like a sleepy kitten. Despite a full shift, she looked rested. White teeth flashed in her lovely tan skin.

"Who is it this time?" Lindsey flopped back on her pillows, a resigned tone in her voice.

"T.D.M., I guess."

"Who?"

"Tall, dark, and mysterious. You know, now you see him,

now you don't. Patti saw a black sports car in the parking lot and headed that way." Shina patted a yawn with dainty fingers.

The arrival of a childishly disappointed Patti broke into their conversation. "I couldn't see if it was our stranger."

"Our stranger? My, she's getting generous," Lindsey said sarcastically.

Shina chimed in, "Tsk, tsk, and after she clearly pointed out she saw him first." She put her elbows on her knees, crossed her hands, and used them to prop up her chin. "Know what, Lindsey? Patti reminds me of a little dog chasing a big car. Once she catches it, what on earth is she going to do? Sit up and beg?"

"No. She will look at T.D.M. and—"

"Who?" Patti looked at her suspiciously.

"Tall, dark, and mysterious," Shina put in.

Lindsey went on as if there had been no aside. "One look from her forget-me-not blue eyes and he will go down for the count."

"I'm not like that," Patti protested, but a slight smirk denied any offense taken. "Besides, how do we expect to get married if we aren't in the right place at the right time?"

"I believe when God wants us to marry, He will let us know," Shina said. "Look at Dr. Hamilton and Jonica. And Dr. Barton and Nancy. They went through hard times but now they're together and happy." She yawned and got off Lindsey's bed. "I have to clean up for supper. Be back soon."

When the door closed behind her, Patti turned her blue gaze directly on her roommate. "Do you believe what she just said?"

Lindsey started to make a wisecrack but an unspoken plea in Patti's face stilled it. "Yes, I do. Don't you?"

"I hope so." She took the spot Shina had just deserted, even the same pose, cupping her rounded chin in her propped-up hands. "It's just that there are so many nice men, especially here at Shepherd of Love. How can we ever know which ones we should marry?"

"You are totally hopeless, Patricia Thompson. First of all, why not wait until you're asked?" Lindsey heartlessly pushed her off the bed. "Go shower and forget it, will you?" Yet she frowned when she caught Patti's faint whisper, "I wish I could," and filed it away for future consideration.

three

If Terence O'Shea hadn't been in a hospital, he would have whistled his way out of the dining room and down the hall to keep his appointment with the board of directors. Instead, he walked more or less circumspectly, although his heart did an Irish jig and a lilt crept into his voice when he said "good morning" to those he met.

The sight of a woman's face hadn't stirred him like this since his senior year in college. Ever since his roommate had eloped with Terence's girlfriend, he had kept women at a distance. How, in the twinkling moments following the collision, had a red-headed nurse with golden freckles and changeable hazel eyes made such an impression? Her friends had been attractive, too. Yet only Nurse Lindsey Best had kindled a spark in the wary heart he had doubted would ever love again. "Two moving objects meet with force," he muttered. Had they ever! He chuckled. It was a wonder he hadn't fallen as well. Arms swinging free, Terence mulled over the last few minutes. He had wanted the chaplain's job before he came; now, God willing, he intended to have it if it were in his power.

The thought firmed his lips and grayed his eyes. He forced his attention to the coming interview. A silent prayer winged its way upward. *According to Thy will.*

Outside the hospital director's office where the interview would be held, Terence read the inscription on the door. *Thy word is a lamp unto my feet, and a light unto my path* (Psalm 119:105). The familiar verse brought back bittersweet memories of a small boy at his mother's knee, chin on his hand, adoring gaze turned toward the frail woman who smiled down at him. He tightened his lips. This was no time

27

for reminiscing. Taking another deep breath and slowly exhaling, he stepped inside.

"Are you Mr. O'Shea?" a pleasant-faced woman asked.

"That I am." He smiled.

"I'm afraid I have disappointing news for you." She sounded genuinely regretful. "The board is eager to interview you, but they would like Nicholas Fairchild, the hospital founder, to be in on the selection. He was unexpectedly called out of town on business. The chairman would like to reschedule you for tomorrow afternoon at two. Will that be convenient?" She laughed. "There, don't I sound efficient? The hospital director never uses a secretary as a buffer, preferring to be available to staff at any time, but he isn't here just now."

"You do—and tomorrow will be fine." Terence's heart was heavy. Was this a polite brush-off? Or a stall to give them more time to consider someone else? Insisting on the legendary Fairchild's presence was calling in the big guns, but Terence could do nothing about it.

"They really do want to see you, Mr. O'Shea," the woman told him.

"I'm glad." He smiled and went out, wondering how he could wait another day and a half. The smile changed to a grimace. This could be another of the Lord's lessons in teaching him patience, which he knew he sorely needed.

&

The following afternoon when he entered the hospital director's office, the secretary's desk was empty. This time Terence noted the simple but tasteful furnishings in the office. Paneled walls and muted carpeting paled into insignificance next to the large open window's spectacular view of Puget Sound and the snow-capped Olympics.

A keen-eyed man rose from a chair behind a practical desk. He held out his hand. "Thanks for coming, Mr. O'Shea. Sorry we had to postpone our meeting." He introduced the other four members: two men and two women. All appeared alert and observant. Last of all, he turned to the scholarly looking older man next to him. "Mr. Fairchild, Terence O'Shea."

So this was the man God had directed to build Shepherd of Love Hospital! In spite of Fairchild's white-streaked hair, Terence felt he understood why God had picked him. Keen intelligence shone from the blue eyes. Compassion and strength lined the austere face.

Terence found himself measured as never before in his entire life. He bore the scrutiny with head up and fast-beating heart. Without being told, he knew no matter what the rest of the board thought, Nicholas Fairchild must be satisfied or he had no chance of being asked to take over as hospital chaplain.

"Sit down," the chairman invited. "We'll get right to our interview. We are particularly eager to fill the chaplaincy because of an unusual circumstance at Shepherd of Love just now. Our hospital director recently suffered a stroke. Our specialists feel he will regain full health, but of course it will take time." He rested his elbows on the desk and methodically fitted his fingers together. "We haven't yet selected an acting director, but that's another matter entirely, one that only affects you indirectly."

A barrage of questions followed, starting with, "What brought you to Shepherd of Love? You have been out of the country, haven't you?"

"Yes. I came home when my father's health worsened."

Compassion showed in the board members' faces. "Is it serious?"

"Enough that I don't want to be thousands of miles away." Terence felt a muscle twitch in his cheek. "In spite of a history of rheumatoid arthritis, Dad did fine living alone until just a few weeks ago. This time when it flared up, it brought complications."

"There are always care centers," Fairchild suggested.

"Not for Dad," Terence retorted, feeling like a pinned

butterfly. "Mom died when I was a child. Dad became mother as well as father. Unless it comes to the point where I can no longer give him the quality of care he needs, Dad and I will remain a team."

"Don't you have siblings who could care for him?" the chairman asked. "It seems too bad you were called home from such a distance."

"Oh, I do have siblings." Terence laughed out loud. "Four older sisters, all married. I was the baby of the family, born after my sisters married and moved away. They are scattered from Albuquerque to Akron. Dad still lives on the family farm near Redmond. I'd like to keep him there as long as possible."

"Suppose you marry?" one of the women wanted to know.

What a strange interview! Terence couldn't tell if the questions were meant to needle or test him. He hesitated. If he'd been asked that a half-hour earlier his answer would have been a direct, "I'm fancy free." Now the vision of a red-haired nurse persisted in knocking at the door of his mind. He slammed it shut and shrugged. "I won't worry about it until the time comes, if it does."

The finality in his voice effectively closed the subject. Terence sent a lightning glance around the circle of watching faces. The approval in their expressions gave him the courage to plunge to the heart of things. "To reply to your first question, I believe my coming to Shepherd of Love may be an answer to prayer. I asked for a job within commuting distance of the farm. The next day an old friend who 'just happened' to know your present chaplain's wife 'just happened' to drop by. She 'just happened' to mention your chaplain's plans to retire." He felt again the thrill that had come when he first heard of the job.

"I'd be interested to know," Fairchild stated, "why you say it may be an answer to prayer rather than stating positively you believe it is."

Terence knew his astonishment at the astute question

must show. "I don't have the audacity to presume to know the mind or will of God until it is revealed and confirmed," he said. "In this case, by your receiving the impression I am the right one for the job." For a moment he feared he had gone too far. If so, so be it. He would not sail under false colors even to get a job he more and more longed to have. Everything about the hospital had impressed him favorably so far, including these men and women who helped shape its policies and practices.

Fairchild just smiled. Terence had the feeling he hadn't struck out, but gained at least first base.

The chairman hemmed and hawed a bit, looking embarrassed. "Would you be willing to come on a trial basis? For a month or two, maybe more?"

Terence's spirits, which had steadily soared throughout the stiff examination, sank at the suggestion. The board members evidently did not yet feel sure of him or such an offer wouldn't have been made. In the little pool of silence that fell, he considered. Should he accept the half-loaf, when he had hoped for a whole? Doing so meant having time to prove himself. On the other hand, if he gave two to three months to Shepherd of Love and they decided in favor of another candidate, where did that leave Terence O'Shea? Right where he was now—jobless and waiting for a door to open.

The chairman cleared his throat for the second time and fidgeted in his chair. "Nicholas is at a disadvantage concerning your application, Mr. O'Shea." His face reddened. "It appeared fine when it came in so we sent it on to Personnel to be kept on hand with others." He laughed shamefacedly. "I've been known to misplace, even lose things."

"Wasn't everything in order?" Terence interrupted.

"Very much so." The chairman squirmed. "In fact, we felt good about you."

"I don't understand." A bewildered Terence shook his head.

"Neither do we," one of the other men solemnly said. He lowered his voice as if afraid of being overheard. "A break-in occurred in the personnel department between the time the office closed last night and when it reopened this morning."

"What has that to do with me?"

"When we sent for your file this morning for Nicholas, it was missing."

"Missing?" Terence exploded from his chair, then sank back in response to the chairman's wave. "Why would anyone want my application?"

"It isn't just yours," the chairman explained. "Actually, it may still be somewhere in Personnel. Right now, the employees are attempting to clean up the mess left by the intruder or intruders. Employee information is normally computerized. However, Personnel has been shorthanded. Applications received in the past few weeks were temporarily dropped into file folders to be held pending action. The material from those folders was dumped in a jumble on the floor."

"Sounds more like a malicious prank than a planned theft," Terence observed. He frowned and his brows formed a straight line above his intense eyes. "Yet why would anyone take the risk of discovery just to play a trick?"

"Do you know of anyone who might want to learn more about you or the work you were doing?" Fairchild asked. "Do you have enemies?"

Terence shook his head. "No—not that I know of."

One of the women moved restlessly, as if reminding them they were there to select a chaplain, not solve a mystery. "Will you recap your experience for Nicholas, please?"

Terence obligingly began to relate the basic information his application contained. "Degree in Engineering from the University of Washington."

The chairman stopped him. "You didn't actually pursue that profession."

"No. I worked at Boeing for a couple of years and found myself restless." Terence stared out the window, remembering the dissatisfaction with his job. "I felt like a cog that could be replaced by any number of qualified men or women. Dad and I made it a matter of prayer. Over a period of time, I realized I wanted to make a difference in people's lives beyond being part of making bigger and better airplanes." His voice turned husky. "I never heard angel voices or saw visions, but gradually I felt led to the ministry."

"You entered seminary?" Fairchild inquired, an unreadable expression on his intent face.

"Yes. I enjoyed preaching but unlike my fellow students, had little desire for a church of my own. I longed to serve, yet found myself in a web of uncertainty, unable to discover what God had in mind for me. He didn't seem to be speaking. Or I may have been so engrossed in myself, I wasn't hearing." He sighed. "It was a distressing time."

"I can see it would be." The conversation narrowed into a dialogue between Terence and Nicholas Fairchild.

"I approached a professor who never hesitated to give himself to the seminary students, and I laid my dilemma before him. I'll never forget his piercing, wintry gaze when he asked, 'Are you willing to go anywhere, do anything, be anybody God asks?' I hesitated, examined my soul, and told him I thought so.

"His giant fist crashed to his scarred desk. 'Mr. O'Shea,' he said. 'Until you can come in here, stand before God and me, and shout *yes* at the top of your lungs, I have no time to waste on you.'"

Terence swiped at his eyes to rid himself of the blur the vivid scene brought.

"What did you do?" the obviously enthralled listeners wanted to know.

His voice dropped to a whisper. "Fasted and prayed for three days and nights."

"And?" Fairchild barked, his voice far different from his

usual quiet tone.

A great laugh escaped from Terence's constricted throat. "I charged into the professor's office like a raging tiger and bellowed *yes!*"

Sympathetic chuckles greeted the story of his outburst.

Terence went on. "The professor leaped from his chair with such exuberance it crashed to the floor behind him. His hand shot out, gripped mine, and he said, 'Now I can help you.' And he did."

"By finding you a chaplain's job on a medical mission ship to Haiti," the chairman put in.

"Right." Terence felt himself come alive. "I wouldn't trade the experience for anything. Just being there for a staff who gave one hundred and ten percent of their time, energy, and love meant everything. I saw them offer hope to men, women, and children who had none. Every patient meant a new challenge, a new opportunity. I learned rudimentary lay medical procedures and assisted in physical healing as well as spiritual. More than ever, I realized how the two must work hand in hand."

"Which is exactly our goal," Fairchild murmured.

"I know," Terence softly said. "That's why I want to be part of Shepherd of Love." He bowed his head, but not before he saw the flash of approval in the hospital founder's blue eyes.

After a moment of profound silence, the interview ended unexpectedly. Fairchild turned to the chairman. "I believe we have heard enough, unless you or the others have further questions?"

Terence could tell nothing from his noncommittal statement.

When the board indicated they had nothing more to ask, the chairman said, "We will be in touch, Mr. O'Shea. Thank you for coming." He casually added, "Be thinking about the temporary offer, will you?"

Standard dismissal, Terence thought. In a few days he would receive a polite letter thanking him again, perhaps even praising his qualifications, but stating another had been chosen. Sadness filled him. Even though he had prayed for God's will to be done, he found it hard to understand. The chaplaincy offered work he loved, the means by which he could care for Dad. A fresh pang went through him. His father's farseeing eyes would ferret out his only son's disappointment, but how could he tell Dad? Should he have accepted the temporary offer when it was first mentioned?

He stubbornly shook his head. No. He hadn't felt any leading to do so and until he did, he could not shackle himself to a position that might in the end be taken from him.

O'Shea pride forced Terence to shake hands all around, thank the men and women for their time, and start out. Just before he reached the door, Fairchild said, "Mr. O'Shea, close the door behind you and wait outside, please."

"Certainly." What now? He stepped through the doorway, into the hall, and pulled the door toward him. The last thing he intended was to eavesdrop, yet just before the door shut, he heard Fairchild's voice. Something told him the older man intended for him to hear.

"I recommend we hire that young man, with no reservations."

Terence tried to control the grin that started in his heart and curled his lips. He leaned against the corridor wall, absently staring at a wall clock a little distance away. A minute passed. Two. Three. Funny. He'd never before noticed how seconds limped into minutes, like patients favoring an injured leg.

"Mr. O'Shea, will you come in again, please?" Fairchild himself opened the door and waited for Terence to enter. "We'd like you to be our chaplain. No probationary period. I'll walk with you to Personnel so they can get the necessary information to put into the computer." His eyes twinkled. "We're taking no chances on losing you a second time."

"Congratulations, Chaplain O'Shea. We know you will

be an asset to Good Shepherd." The chairman beamed, as did the others. Another round of handshakes, and Terence silently accompanied his new friend down the hall.

Fairchild chuckled. "Go ahead and say it, son. You'll burst if you don't."

"I was just wondering—"

"—what I said after the door closed." Another chuckle rumbled deep in his throat. "Terence, no one who talks with you for any length of time can fail to see what you are." Laughter died. "Let an old man give you a wee piece of advice. If ever you are in doubt as to what to say to someone in trouble, simply tell them God loves them. Then share what He has done for you. I've found in my three score and ten years those two witnesses to be the most effective way to lead folks to the Lord, comfort them, or make them know life is worth living."

"You remind me of my father," Terence choked out from behind an obstruction in his throat that felt bigger than the Rock of Gibraltar. "I hope he can meet you someday. You'd like him."

"I already like his son," Fairchild said. "Very much."

Terence couldn't answer.

When he finished the necessary paperwork and came out of Personnel, Terence was surprised to find his sponsor waiting for him in the hall. "Mr. Fairchild, I just don't know how to thank you," Terence blurted out, feeling more like a ten-year-old schoolboy in the presence of a favorite teacher than a thirty-year-old, full-fledged chaplain.

"Simply serve Shepherd of Love with all you have." A poignant light softened the keenness of his blue eyes. He shook Terence's hand once more, started off, then turned and wistfully said, "Terence, there is one other thing."

"Anything."

"Call me Nicholas. We're brothers in Him, you know." Fairchild smiled and walked away, leaving the new chaplain feeling he had just been blessed.

four

A dark figure nervously walked the floor of a musty room in a deserted, falling-to-ruin warehouse. Barren except for a battered desk that held a telephone, the worn boards groaned in protest at being disturbed. Fear like a living thing gripped the pacer. Why didn't he call? The prearranged time had long since passed.

Seconds dragged into minutes. His nerves twanged. He felt sweat form and bead in great drops. At last the phone issued a low scream. The instrument's volume had been carefully turned down, but even the faint noise further jangled his frayed nerves, sounding hollow in the vacant building.

"Yes? Yes. It's about time." A furtive glance around the empty room assured the speaker he could not be overheard, except by a multitude of spiders spinning their death trap webs in the corners.

"It went as planned." A smile of triumph touched the speaker's face. One hand closed in a convulsive grip. A long list of instructions poured into his ear; he listened with a brain made keen by waiting, interrupting only occasionally with a few grunts.

"Got that?" the man on the other end of the line barked. His tone demanded total obedience and left no room for incompetence or failure.

"Got it."

A click, then a dial tone. The dark figure unplugged the phone and carelessly stuffed it in the bottom drawer of the old desk. Relief came like a shower. If everything went as well as it had so far. . . Again, one hand shut in a gesture of victory. It wouldn't be long now.

Terence O'Shea sang all the way from Shepherd of Love
Hospital in Seattle across the floating bridge that spanned
Lake Washington, then north on Interstate 405 to the
Redmond exit. Once off the freeway, he curbed his impa-
tience to reach the farm and slowed his station wagon to
accommodate the country roads. His heart swelled and he
broke off singing as he thought, *I missed western Washington while I was gone—but I didn't realize how much until I
came back.*

Although he'd been born in San Francisco, Terence's
images of the steep hills, trolley cars, Fisherman's Wharf,
and Chinatown came from adult visits rather than childhood memories. With the birth of their fifth child and only
son, Shane and Moira O'Shea followed their hearts to Washington where they purchased the rundown farm near
Redmond. Terence grew up surrounded by hills and for-
ests, meadows and gardens. He fished in the stream that ran
through their property, and flat on his back beneath pine
and firs, he watched cloud pictures form between the green
needles. He tolerated the cows and chickens he helped care
for as part of his chores, but he genuinely loved the wild
rabbits, squirrels, and occasional coyote or deer that visited
the farm. Tragedy had touched him when he was ten and
his mother died in a car accident—but Dad had always been
there: father, confidante, his son's best friend outside of God.

Now Terence sighed. He carefully swung into the long
driveway leading to the old white farmhouse. "Never
thought I'd miss the moo of cows or the cackling of chickens," he admitted with a grin. It died when he braked to a
stop in front of the house. How long could he and Dad stay
here? In the short time since he returned from Haiti, he'd
made giant inroads on the weeds threatening to choke out
the gardens but he couldn't keep it up, care for Dad, and
still do a good job at the hospital. The thought of selling the
place made him blink. Could they find another alternative?

"I know You will provide, God," he murmured. A few long strides took him across the porch and through the front door. "Dad?" He sniffed. "Hey, you're up and cooking."

"You bet I am!"

"That's not the voice of an invalid," Terence teased when he reached the spotless white kitchen with its colorful tile floor.

"So who's an invalid?" Dad set an enormous bowl of potato salad on the round table in the window corner. The blue-checked tablecloth already held two place settings, plus bread, butter, and condiments.

Pain had lined Shane O'Shea's face and streaked his mahogany hair with silver, but it had not dimmed the eyes that were even bluer than his son's. The rheumatoid arthritis that stiffened his joints could not touch his magnificent soul. Shane put a plate of sliced tomatoes on the table, then turned back to the stove and took up fresh green beans cooked with onion and thick slices of turkey ham. The gnarled hands were a little awkward, and Terence itched to help. He knew, though, that his father wanted and needed to be allowed to do all he could.

"Looks wonderful and I'm starved. Oh, Dad, I got the job." He headed for the kitchen sink to wash his hands.

Shane's laugh rumbled deep in his big chest. "As if I didn't know the moment you stepped onto the porch! No man has such a spring in his step if he's just been turned down or passed over." His eyes gleamed. "Let's have the blessing, boy, and you can tell me about it. My turn, I think."

Terence nodded and bowed his head. As always, he was touched by the simple words of thankfulness his father expressed to the God who ruled their lives. "So what did you do today other than cook for your starving son?" he inquired. "You aren't overdoing, are you?"

"Not at all." Shane cut his meat and looked subdued. "I'm a lot better, so much so I feel ashamed at having interrupted your life by allowing you to come home and care for me."

Terence stopped a forkful of salad halfway to his mouth. "Are you joking? Why should I be off caring for someone else when I can be here eating your cooking and growing excited about this new opportunity?" He ate the bite of salad and grinned. "Your potato salad gets better every time. Dad, you can't believe how right I feel about the chaplaincy. It's as if everything in my life has been directing me to this point." He didn't add the feeling had begun with his chance encounter with Lindsey Best.

Shane visibly relaxed. "I never want to be a burden," he quietly said. "One of these days you'll be finding the right woman and settling down. Never let me stand in the way of your happiness."

A certain wistfulness in his father's voice caused Terence to say, "Suppose we worry about that when it happens." Funny, first the hospital board had been concerned over his love life, and now Dad. He laughed outright. "You aren't going to start sounding like the girls, are you?"

Shane roared and his eyes twinkled. He put on a rich Irish brogue and reminded, "Shure, and what would ye ixpict wi' four colleens, each more happily married than the ither, all longin' for their baby brother to wed?"

A rollicking time of "do you remembers" followed, based on the many and devious ways Terence had outwitted his matchmaking sisters.

"They mean well, boy," Shane finally said.

"I know, but aren't marriages supposed to be made in heaven?"

"True, but they're lived out on earth and your sisters cannot resist putting a hand in. You'll have to admit, the girls they brought around were always nice."

"Who cares, if they're not the one for me?" Terence retorted. He shoved back from the table. "I'm stuffed."

"Too full for apple cobbler ready to come out of the oven?"

"Not I." Terence hastily reversed himself. "I'll fetch it. Getting up and down will furnish a little exercise and make

more room for it." He brought the steaming cobbler, dished
up generous portions, and added a dollop of butter to the
spicy apples and crust. "Dad, I'm really glad to be home—
and I thank God you've improved."

"You know there's no real cure, Terence."

"I know but that doesn't mean there won't be one day. In
the meantime, we're going to do everything possible for
you." His Irish chin set in a fighting line that boded ill for
disease or danger threatening one he loved. He loaded the
dishwasher, still talking. Like the Bests' kitchen, the
O'Sheas had a rocker that symbolized how much wonderful comradeship took place in the big room, and now Shane
sat and rocked, while he thanked God for the light he saw
in his son's face and heard in his voice.

❧

Hours later, Terence stood at the window of his upstairs
bedroom, looking into a glorious night. The desire to be out
in it overrode the more practical need to get a good night's
sleep. He quietly went downstairs, across the porch, and
into the moonlit meadow. The stream he loved gurgled with
joy and reflected the countless, shimmering stars that made
the night sky a thing of wonder. Distant, snow-capped mountains showed between slightly swaying evergreens, eternal,
immutable. A sense of peace pervaded him. Where else on
earth could anyone feel closer to his Creator? At least for
this night, crime and sin in the world seemed far away; the
farm stood strong, a haven of stability in a mad, sometimes
senseless world.

Terence did not go inside until a low keening in the trees
told him the night wind had risen, and it became too chilly
for comfort to a man standing motionless, even though he
gazed on incomparable beauty. He quietly made his way
back across the porch and up the stairs. No sound came from
his father's room until Terence inched his bedroom door
open and stepped inside. Then the greeting came, the words
he'd unconsciously waited for and heard thousands of times,

no matter what time he got home.

"Good night, boy."

"Good night, Dad." He closed the door. Dad had been keeping watch. All was well. "Just like You, Father," he whispered into the cool air of his room, glad to be back where he could sleep with the window wide open and gaze upwards at the moon and stars.

❧

A few days later, all hospital personnel who could be spared from the wards and offices received a summons to a general staff meeting. Scuttlebutt had it both the new hospital chaplain and acting hospital director had been selected. Patti, Shina, Lindsey, and the rest of the hospital knew Terence O'Shea had been unanimously chosen to fill the chaplaincy but speculation as to the new temporary director ran like spilled oil. For once, Dame Rumor failed to discover and pass on the news.

The three nurses filed into the auditoriumlike room used for such gatherings and found seats together. "There's Nicholas Fairchild," Patti whispered. She dug her elbows into Lindsey and Shina, who flanked her on either side. "See, with the directors? Oh, there's Terence." She stood and waved. Before Lindsey could tell her to sit down and stop acting like a beauty queen waving to everyone from a parade float, Patti gulped and added in a loud whisper, "My goodness, girls, it's *him*!"

"I don't see anyone special," Shina said.

"Him, who? Besides, the correct grammar is *he*, not *him*." Lindsey succeeded in getting Patti back into her seat.

"*He, him*, who cares." Patti clutched her friend's arms with unexpectedly strong fingers. "Him. You know. T.D.M."

"Tall, dark, and mysterious?" Shina craned her neck in a vain effort to see past much taller persons laughing and swarming into the seats in front of them.

"Really?" Lindsey straightened her tired spine out of its slump. "You don't think—"

Patti clasped her hands and gave a deep blissful sigh. "I don't think anything. I just know he's even more gorgeous than before. It's positively unfair for any one man to be so good-looking."

Lindsey silently echoed her friend's sentiments when Nicholas, the board of directors, Terence O'Shea, and the tall, dark stranger walked onto the platform at the front of the room. The same thrill she hadn't been able to identify the first time she saw the spectacularly handsome man fluttered her pulse and quickened her heartbeat. A second feeling, even more elusive, brushed gossamer wings against her mind. A disturbed feeling that something wasn't right haunted her.

Nicholas Fairchild stepped to the microphone. "Welcome and thank you for coming," he said simply. The overhead lights silvered his gray hair. "I won't keep you long. Many of you need to get back to our patients. I just want to introduce our new chaplain and acting director."

In a mental daze, Lindsey watched Terence O'Shea step forward when beckoned. She heard his solemn voice vowing to give his best to Shepherd of Love. Before he returned to his seat amidst thunderous applause, she noticed his eyes shone more blue than gray, but she quickly turned her attention back to Nicholas Fairchild.

"As you all know, our hospital director will need some months to recuperate. We have considered several candidates, all highly qualified. I'm happy to introduce to you Dr. Bartholomew Keppler, although he says he prefers to be called Bart." A ripple of laughter swept through the group and Lindsey sucked in her breath. T.D.M.—Dr. Keppler— stepped forward.

"Along with Mr. O'Shea, I pledge to faithfully carry out my duties. I will make sure Shepherd of Love Hospital is given the homage and loyalty I feel it deserves." He spread his hands deprecatingly. "Stepping into your beloved director's place won't be easy. I'll need all your cooperation." He smiled with a flash of teeth so white he could, Lindsey thought, obtain work advertising toothpaste. She bit her lips at the irreverent thought.

After a few more remarks, he smiled again and sat down in a din that showed how impressed the staff had been.

"Isn't he won-der-ful?" Bright pink spots flared in Patti's clear skin.

"He hasn't done anything yet but talk," Lindsey said perversely.

Shina giggled but Patti glared. "Don't be horrid, Lindsey Best. Come on. Let's go wish him—them—well." She practically dragged her friends up the aisle. Shina rolled her eyes in exasperation and submitted. Lindsey hung back a few steps.

"We just want to welcome you both," Patti said when they reached her prey. She quickly introduced herself, Lindsey, and Shina to Dr. Keppler. "I suppose you've already met Terence—Chaplain O'Shea," she added.

"Actually, I haven't. I arrived just before the meeting started." Keppler held out his hand. "Welcome to my hospital, Chaplain."

My hospital. Not *the* hospital or Shepherd of Love. Lindsey caught a curious terrier-brightness in the new chaplain's eyes when he said, "Thanks," and took the extended hand. It reminded her of the look in a dog's eyes just before he unearthed and pounced on a rat. Laughter like carbonated water bubbled inside her.

She managed to say hello, but her voice shook slightly from controlled mirth. Another minute and she'd laugh out loud. "I have to go, Patti," she said. "Are you coming?"

"Y—yes." The reluctant agreement sounded dragged out of her roommate and the minute they got out of earshot, she demanded, "Well?"

Lindsey hesitated, knowing Patti wanted a glowing response but not able to give it. "As I said earlier, he hasn't done anything yet but talk. I'll reserve judgment for a while, if it's all right with you."

Shina glanced back over her shoulder. "Me, too." Her midnight-black eyes looked solemn. "I think I like Terence better."

"For goodness' sake, why?" Patti stared at the tiny nurse.

"I know it sounds silly, but I read a Western novel once and the villain's name was Black Bart—"

"Shina Ito, that's positively unchristian! Taking a dislike to someone because of his name? I never heard of such a thing." Patti's face turned red.

"She didn't say she disliked him and neither did I." Lindsey poured oil on the troubled waters. "Why the instant defense, anyway?"

Quick tears moistened Patti's long lashes. "I'm sorry. It's just that the Shepherd of Love staff has always been united and I don't want it to change. It's bad enough losing our director and chaplain and having to get used to new people. I just want everyone to be happy and like each other."

Lindsey and Shina exchanged glances. What a child Patti was, in spite of being a terrific nurse and twenty-four years old! Yet that very trait made her lovable.

"You're right, Patti. I'm being unreasonable," Shina apologized. She slipped one arm under Patti's, the other through the crook made by Lindsey's elbow. "I have time for juice before going back on duty. How about you?"

Patti nodded. "Lindsey?"

She started to say she needed to sleep but then decided a few minutes less rest wouldn't kill her. "Sure." They sauntered down the hall, differences forgotten or at least shelved for a time.

"The Three Musketeers, as I live and breathe." Terence O'Shea greeted them at the dining room door. "May I have the pleasure of your company?"

"Of course." Patti never let her admiration for one eligible male rule out spending time with others. Yet Lindsey had to admit her blonde friend was neither shallow nor a flirt. She simply liked people and they adored her. Patti's sunshiny personality warmed all those around her, although she always insisted Lindsey was the one who brought happiness to others.

Four tall lemonades before them, talk naturally turned to Dr. Keppler.

"What did you think of him?" Patti boldly asked the question Lindsey had secretly hoped she would.

Terence sipped his icy drink. "Evidently he is eminently qualified. Gossip has it Dr. Keppler's credentials are as impeccable as his clothing."

Why did a slight frown crease the new chaplain's broad forehead?

Patti played with a straw. "It will be interesting to meet his wife."

"I don't think he's married."

Again Lindsey sensed a certain hesitancy in Terence's voice. Perhaps he had also decided to reserve judgment on the new acting director. She finished her lemonade and stood. "I can hear my bed calling. See you all later." She started out, glad to be free of the incessant chattering about "Black Bart" that buzzed throughout the room.

Terence caught her at the door, looked both ways, and lowered his voice. "Lindsey, what do you think of him?" His steady gaze, more gray than blue, searched her. "I'll wager you're a good judge of people."

"Usually." She hesitated. "Let's see. He's tall. Dark. Mysterious. The answer to many a maiden's prayer," she flippantly admitted.

"Yours, too?" He stood curiously still.

She sensed more behind the question than idle chit-chat, and she opened her mouth in denial. Yet, truthfully, each time she saw Dr. Keppler her pulse beats increased. "I don't know," she confessed. "There's something about him. . ." Her voice faded.

A shadow swept the last of the blue from Terence O'Shea's

watching eyes. Surprise? Disappointment? A combination of both? "I'd best let you go get your rest," he told her and turned away.

She wanted to call him back. *Don't be a fool,* she told herself. *He's just a nice man, nothing more. Why should you care what he thinks?* Yet Lindsey watched Terence walk down the corridor, feeling she had lost something precious, something she could not even name.

five

"What do you have to report?"

"Nothing. It's too soon." The speaker clutched the phone, hating the empty warehouse and the metallic taste of fear.

"Don't make excuses."

"You want me to risk blowing my cover?"

A curse shivered in the listener's ear.

"Give me time," the low voice protested.

"Time is what we don't have. Either get results or get out and we'll put someone in who will."

"Impossible!"

The only answer was the click of the phone and then the buzzing dial tone.

⋆

For the first few months after the advent of the new chaplain and acting hospital director, life and healing continued as usual in the Shepherd of Love.

"Not true," Lindsey muttered. Terry O'Shea's broad grin when they met never failed to bring a smile and Bart—she stopped short. Why had he singled her out, when not only Patti but practically every single, unmarried female employee in the hospital made no secret his attentions would be welcome?

"Why me?" she asked Shina one Friday morning when Patti was on duty. The nurses sat curled up on either end of Lindsey's sofa. Shina looked like a Japanese doll in the kimono outfit she liked to wear off duty. "It can't be because I don't fall at his feet and worship. Neither do you."

"Don't sell yourself short, Lindsey." Shina's dark eyes shone with fun.

"Short I am not, small, dark, and beautiful. How come he

48

avoids you like the Bubonic plague?"

"He didn't at first." Mischief danced in Shina's face. "He asked if I'd like to take in a concert. I thanked him, said I was sorry, but I planned to be married."

"Shina Ito, that's an outright lie. You're no more engaged than I am!" Lindsey couldn't believe it. Like Lindsey, Shina stood for the truth, the whole truth, and nothing but the truth.

"I didn't say I was engaged." She smirked. "I said I planned to be married. I do, someday, when God sends the right man along." A trill of laughter showed how delighted she felt to put one over on observant Lindsey.

"Well, I never. All this time I didn't think you had a devious bone in your body." Lindsey stared. "Just for curiosity's sake, why did you turn him down?"

Shina's laughter died. "I don't know." Her silky eyebrows drew together in a straight line. "He's handsome, courteous, dedicated—Mr. Perfect, as far as anyone knows."

"Do you know differently?"

"No." She folded her hands into the wide kimono sleeves. "I guess I just can't forget the villain in that silly book. Until the last chapter, no one knew he was anything but respectable, but it turned out he led an outlaw gang that plundered and left havoc in their wake. I've even prayed about my aversion. Patti's right, you know. Distrusting someone because of his name is totally unchristian." She sighed. "You were out with him last night. What's he really like, other than attentive?" She sent a meaningful glance at the enormous bouquet of yellow, gold, and orange dahlias and mums on a nearby table.

"I don't know," Lindsey admitted. "He's asked me out so many times I finally ran out of excuses. Besides, yesterday he stopped me in the hall and wanted to know why I kept turning him down."

"Why did you?"

"Who knows? Maybe because I read the same Western you did."

Shina's soft laugh rewarded her, but Lindsey grimaced. "It didn't help when he asked pointblank if I found him repulsive."

Shina sat up straight and her mouth dropped open. "What did you do?"

"What does any dumbfounded person do? I just shook my head." She paused, remembering the triumph that had showed on the handsome face.

"Don't stop now." Shina ordered.

"Dr. Keppler flashed his famous smile and said, 'Good. I'll pick you up at seven. Don't claim you have to work. I checked the schedule.'" Her friend gasped but Lindsey went on. "You haven't heard anything yet. He started away, turned on his heel, and said, 'You'll want to dress up. I have reservations at the Space Needle restaurant.'"

"Really? My goodness, I take a day off to visit my parents and look what happens. What did you wear?" A cloud came to her face. "Does Patti know?"

"I wore the turquoise sheath I bought for last year's staff Christmas party. Patti helped me get ready." Lindsey knew her troubled feelings reflected in her face. "I saw it bothered her, but she's a good sport. She kept telling me I'd have a wonderful time and she insisted on lending me that short fake fur jacket of hers. Good thing, too. These fall evenings are getting chillier every night."

After a long, silent moment she added, "The weird thing is, I did have a good time. Bart Keppler is everything an escort should be. He knows all the niceties, such as having me tell him what I wanted before he ordered for me, serving me bread, all the stuff Patti dotes on. He's sophisticated, charming, able to make even my tired pulse beat a little faster." She yawned and snuggled deeper into the sofa's welcoming depths.

"And today the gorgeous flowers came."

"I'm too comfortable to move but if you want gorgeous, look in the fridge."

Shina uncurled herself and ducked into the kitchenette. She reappeared a moment later carrying a clear florist's box, a delighted expression on her face. "Ooo, they are exquisite." She opened the box and gently withdrew a spray of dainty white orchids held with a knot of silver ribbon. "Lindsey, Dr. Keppler must really want to make an impression." She cocked her shining dark head to one side. "Did he ask you out again?"

"For tomorrow."

"Are you going?" Shina eyed her curiously.

"Yes, but I won't be alone with him." She grinned at Shina's mystified look. "At breakfast yesterday, Terence O'Shea put in a bid. He, Patti, and I had been talking about the outdoors. We told him how much we loved to hike. He promptly said the nights have been cold enough on Mount Rainier to make the leaves spectacular and would we go with him on Saturday. No glacier climbing, or anything like that. Just some of the forest and meadow trails. You're invited, too. Terence said, 'Don't forget to ask your pretty friend.'"

Shina blushed. "How did Dr. Keppler get in on it?" She made a wry face. "I just can't bring myself to call him Bart."

"A psychiatrist would have a field day with you," Lindsey callously told her. "Anyway, when I mentioned the trip, Bart promptly said he'd been wanting to hike the mountain and see the color. He added that if we didn't mind, he would join us. Want to come? If it will make you more comfortable, we'll ask one of your stag line to even the number."

"Thanks, but I'm on duty." Shina took the orchids back to the fridge and returned to her place on the sofa. "Lindsey, how do you think this is going to work out?" Uncertainty lurked in her dark eyes. "Dr. Keppler has dated Patti several times. I'm afraid she's infatuated, if not genuinely in love with him."

"I hope not, but I agree. With every other man she admired, Patti always chattered incessantly about how wonderful he was. Not this time. Except for when he first came, she hasn't mentioned him. If his name happens to come up, she changes the subject. It really concerns me."

Shina folded her arms back into her kimono sleeves. "On the other hand," she slowly said, "it might be the best thing in the world. If he has made her think she is special to him—and men like him usually do—the fact he took you to such an expensive place and sent flowers is bound to set her wondering. Those outsize blue eyes may appear candid and childlike, but they hide a keen brain and are a lot more observant than people who don't know her well ever guess. A whole day spent with him, you, and Terence may enlighten her a lot, especially if Dr. Keppler can't resist the opportunity to impress you."

"You may be right, but I wish he hadn't asked to go." Normally cheerful, Lindsey knew she sounded sullen, but she didn't care one bit.

"We may be doing him a grave injustice," Shina remarked. "Perhaps he simply likes women and is trying not to play favorites."

"Maybe he's just trying to date as many as he can in the time he's here."

"Any idea how long that might be?"

Lindsey remained quiet so long Shina repeated the question.

"I don't know. Bart said last night he heard the director wasn't doing quite so well as before. Evidently the board of directors indicated Bart might be needed here longer than they thought at first."

The sound of the door opening cut short their conversation. Patti, perky in an orchid pantsuit uniform, bounced in. Her smile-wreathed face successfully masked whatever troubles or hurts she might secretly carry. "No fair, Shina. I'll bet Lindsey's told you all about her date." She dropped into a recliner and tilted both her chin and the leg rest skyward. "Well, she can just start over."

"What are you doing off duty, anyway?" Lindsey wanted to know.

"For some strange reason Outpatient got really quiet. The charge nurse gave me the afternoon off. She said I deserved it, what with the extra shifts I worked when she had to be gone. Now give," she sternly ordered.

In a surprising few words Lindsey gave the gist of her evening, omitting the conversation in the hospital corridor. Shina brought out the florist's box. If Patti felt envious, she hid it well. "Whew, orchids even. He said it to me with gardenias." She giggled and her friends exchanged a glance of relief. This was more like the old Patti.

"Did Dr. Keppler tell you he'd be joining us tomorrow?" Lindsey cut to the heart of the situation and watched the blonde nurse carefully.

"Uh huh. Nice, huh?" She couldn't have sounded less caring than if she'd learned one of the stuffed animals from Pediatrics was accompanying them. "When do we leave? Shina, are you coming?"

"Early." "No, I'm working," they chorused. Shina rose. "Time for lunch."

"Not I." Lindsey yawned. "I had a huge breakfast. I traded for swing shift and need some beauty sleep before heading to surgery, my home away from home."

"Think it will help?" Patti teased.

Again Shina and Lindsey's glances met. Shina gave a quick thumbs-up behind Patti's back before she went out. Nothing too serious could be weighing on their friend's mind when she joked like that.

Lindsey had no time to brood over undercurrents that evening. After a quiet afternoon, surgery turned into a madhouse, one of those occasions the staff dreaded yet knew inevitably came. "Road construction, big events at both the Kingdome and Seattle Center, and impatient people don't mix," the chief surgeon announced when two more accident cases came up from Emergency. "Neither do driving, booze, and tailgating. We'll be lucky to save this one."

Lindsey blinked hard and took three deep breaths. Her righteous anger helped restore her control. The woman on the table whose life hung in precarious balance had not been drinking. Neither had her husband. Yet as so often happened, their compliance with every law of the road failed to protect them. The other driver's blood alcohol had tested far above the legal limit, accounting for his careening the wrong way onto a one-way street. His truck struck the older couple's subcompact head-on; he escaped unhurt. The husband ended up with minor injuries but the wife had received serious head wounds.

Please, God, help us do our best. How many times had she offered the prayer? How many times had she privately agonized, even while keeping hands steady and mind alert to anticipate a surgeon's needs? They seldom had to ask for an instrument when Nurse Lindsey Best stood by the operating table. No thought of self or the passing of time intruded.

When the last patient had been cared for and sent to ward or ICU, Lindsey glanced at the clock. After midnight. Bone weary, still she rejoiced. Thanks to God and a dedicated staff, no sheet-covered patient would go from Surgery to the morgue this night.

Lindsey shed her soiled scrubs, washed her hands, and climbed into clean clothes, feeling hollow from skipping supper. She stepped into the hall and found Terence O'Shea waiting for her. "You here? Is our hike off?"

"That's what I wanted to ask you. Will you be too tired?" He looked far older than his years, his jaw set in a grim line. "It's been quite a night."

"I'll be fine." She yawned. "What's it like in Emergency?"

"Bad. Two DOAs—teenagers on their way home from a victory bash." He sounded depressed. "This is the worst part of my new job, talking with parents whose hearts are breaking. It's so hard to know what to say that can make a difference."

Lindsey laid one hand on his arm. "Just being there to listen may be the best you can offer."

He gratefully covered her hand with his own. "I know. Just the way you're listening to me when I needed to spill out my feelings."

His eyes had gone from stormy gray to gentle blue; something she saw in them caught at her heart. Lindsey smiled. "If we're going hiking tomorrow, no, today, we'd better get some sleep."

"Right." He released her hand. A wary look crept into his steady gaze. "We want to be able to keep up with our acting hospital director." He sounded like a small, subdued boy.

Lindsey impulsively said, "I didn't invite him."

"You didn't?" Terence looked startled.

"He said he wanted to see the leaves and hoped we wouldn't mind if he joined us." She felt herself redden. Why on earth had she felt she needed to explain?

The radiance in the young chaplain's face more than repaid her confusion. "Thanks, Lindsey." He didn't say for what, but his hard grip on her hand made her fingers tingle. "May I see you home?"

She nodded and bit her tongue to keep from blurting out that he sounded like the olden days, when gentlemen quaintly asked permission to accompany young ladies to their dwelling places. Deep inside she liked it. The expression fit him, just like the courteous little bow he always gave women when he met them.

"I'm really looking forward to tomorrow," he told her when they reached her apartment. "It's been several years since I got to do any climbing on our mountain. It's one of the things I missed while I was in—"

"Lindsey, is that you?" Patti flung open the door. "Hi, Terence. We're still on for tomorrow, aren't we? You won't be too tired, Lindsey?" Concern for her roommate warred with eagerness for the outing.

"I'll be fine after a few hours sleep."

Terence laughed, the rollicking laugh that automatically made others smile in sympathy with his exuberance. "I'm out of here. Oh, I think Dr. Keppler said seven? He assumed you'd want to have breakfast here."

"Yes." Patti frowned. "Oh, dear, I meant to pack a lunch."

"You don't have to. Dad volunteered. He's a great cook, so don't stuff down too much breakfast," Terence warned. Crinkles appeared at the corners of his sparkling eyes. "Although if you get as hungry as I do, we'll be more than ready for lunch no matter how much breakfast we eat."

๛

Morning came clear and crisp, Seattle September at its best. Lindsey and Patti donned jeans, tee shirts, heavy socks, and walking shoes. "Which color?" Patti held up red and blue zip-front sweatshirts with hoods. "It's going to be cold this morning."

"Either. I'm wearing navy. It doesn't show the dirt." Lindsey slipped into the fleece-lined garment and caught her hair back into a short ponytail.

"Good idea. I will, too, if you don't mind us looking like the Bobbsey Twins."

"Sure, with me four inches taller and red-haired."

"Hey, you're speaking of the roommate I love." Patti came to the doorway, navy sweatshirt in one hand. "Did God ever make a more beautiful day?"

"It's great, all right." Lindsey ran a lipstick over her mouth and pronounced herself ready.

Terence arrived halfway through breakfast and repeated his warning about not overeating. "Dad outdid himself on lunch," he boasted.

Patti looked at the steaming cinnamon rolls on the buffet and plaintively asked, "You mean I have to turn down a second roll?"

"Third," Lindsey heartlessly reminded her.

"Only if you don't care for nut bread, fried chicken, ripe tomatoes and lettuce from our garden, and juicy peach turnovers that melt in your mouth," Terence solemnly told her. "Dad packed the chicken in ice and we fixed it so I can carry it in my backpack."

"Then I'll pass up seconds. Okay, thirds." Patti grimaced at Lindsey.

"So will I. That sounds wonderful, O'Shea." Dr. Keppler's hearty approval held nothing of patronage. "This is going to be a day to remember. I feel it in my bones." He laughed and his dark eyes shone. In his black sweatshirt and jeans he looked taller and more handsome than ever, but not at all mysterious.

By contrast, Terence's mahogany hair gleamed above a hunter green sweatshirt and khaki pants. He looked far more rested than at midnight the night before and his eyes glowed with anticipation.

Lindsey's heart gave the little lurch she'd experienced before. When Bart smiled that way, she could see why he dazzled Patti. She felt color come to her face and hastily said, "If my esteemed friend is through ogling the cinnamon rolls, we can go."

Terence forestalled a scathing remark from Patti by whispering, "You may have an extra turnover. Dad sent enough so that if we got caught out overnight we wouldn't starve."

A flash of something strangely akin to fear came to Bart's eyes. "There's no danger of such a thing, is there?"

Terence looked surprised. "Of course not. I've hiked the trails for years and we aren't climbing the mountain itself."

"I didn't think so. It's just that there's been some fatal accidents on Mount Rainier recently." The next moment Bart reverted to his usual, suave self, and the hiking party headed out toward Terence's station wagon.

Patti sniffed ecstatically when Terence unlocked the wagon. She announced, "I'm sitting right in front of the lunch. Coming, Bart?" Intent on getting into the rear seat, she didn't notice Keppler's almost imperceptible hesitation, his fleeting glance at Lindsey. The next instant he said,

"Right, Patti," and stepped into the wagon, leaving a disturbed Lindsey to crawl into the front seat. In that split second, she determined to cling to Terence like a leech and give the flirtatious doctor no cause for soulful glances that both attracted and upset her.

six

Terence O'Shea smiled to himself, inordinately pleased at the flicker of annoyance on Lindsey's expressive face. His keen eyes had seen Dr. Keppler's slight hesitation, his fleeting glance toward the surgical nurse, before he climbed into the rear seat of the station wagon next to Patti. A wave of actual dislike for his superior swept through Terence. Remorse followed. Fine thing, the chaplain of a hospital dedicated to Christlike service entertaining the insane and unfounded desire to punch out its hospital director.

He was humbled by the realization of how far short he fell of the man he longed to be. God had a big job on His hands, taming the legendary O'Shea temper that flared without warning, sometimes with disastrous results. There had been enough incidents during Terence's growing-up years to show the futility of settling things with his fists.

"Never refuse to fight when you are in the right," Dad had taught his son. "Just be mindful of three things. First, make sure you are in the right. Second, never allow your opponent the choice of weapons." His blue eyes grew serious. "Third and most important, don't waste your energy on little things. Save it to fight the real battles such as hunger, poverty, prejudice, injustice."

It took time for the hotheaded boy to realize his best defense was a good offense. When verbally attacked, he never backed down. Instead, he folded his arms across his chest, threw back his head—and laughed in his tormentor's face. Nine times out of ten, others around him took it up, to the dismay of the would-be bully. On a few occasions it didn't work and he ending up walloping someone.

His lips twitched at the memory. Each time, it had taken

only one licking to convince his adversary not to cross the invisible line Terence set. He sighed. If only Satan, the greatest adversary, could be whipped once and for all!

Patti's charming voice recalled him to the present when she gave a little bounce on the backseat and said, "I can hardly wait to get to the mountain."

Terence could see her eager face in his rearview mirror. A moment later, he took his gaze from the road and glanced at Lindsey. Patti's anticipation was also reflected in her eyes. How changeable their color! He had seen them brilliant with laughter, darker when she wore yellow, hazel with deep thought. Today they shone green with tiny brown specks. Rich color flowed into her smooth cheeks and her tiny freckles looked golden against her clear skin. His heart thumped. *I like her*, he silently told himself. *I like her height, the way she walks as if she owns the world, her laughing voice, her compassion and caring.*

"You should enjoy the scenery along the way instead of wishing you were there," Lindsey softly said to Patti.

"Yes, mother." Patti didn't sound at all reproved. "Oh, look!" She pointed out the window toward an eagle wheeling in the morning sky. "How free and unshackled. No wonder our country chose the eagle for our national bird." She spoiled the moment by giggling. "I read where they almost selected a turkey. Wouldn't that have been awful?"

A lazy discussion followed, ending when Terence asked, "Bart, have you ever been to Mount Rainier?"

"No. In fact, I'd never been in Washington until this summer."

"How did you happen to choose our state?" Patti wanted to know.

"Heard Shepherd of Love needed an acting director and figured I could do a great deal of good." He broke off and peered from the window. "Is that another eagle?"

Terence heard Lindsey's slight choking sound before Patti exclaimed, "You need a short course in bird-ology. That's not the word, but I can't remember the real one."

"Ornithology," Lindsey supplied.

"Right. Anyway, that's a crow, not an eagle," Patti said. "You have a real treat in store, Bart. Although Lindsey disagrees with me, the very first hike you take on Mount Rainier is the best."

"Why do you think otherwise?" Bart challenged Lindsey.

She stared through the window, and Terence shot her another lightning glance. Her mobile face had taken on a dreaming look. "I'm like my grandmother, I guess. Someone asked her why she bothered to read books a second or even third time. The questioner insisted there was no joy in reading a story when you knew what would happen." A gentle smile curved her lips.

"What did your grandmother say?" Terence inquired. He felt rather than saw her shift her body in the seat belt until she faced him more squarely.

"She said she always enjoyed a journey more when she knew the destination."

"Good for her!" Terence approved. His merry laugh rang out.

"I guess she does have a point," Patti conceded. "If we didn't know how great it was on Mount Rainier we probably wouldn't be going."

"We could take someone else's word," Bart told her. "As we have to do with the Almighty. I mean, none of us have seen or heard for ourselves."

Why should the simple statement make Terence's hackles rise? What the self-invited hiking guest said was often true. Or was it an undercurrent of amusement in the smooth voice that annoyed him more than what Bart said? Unwilling to comment for fear he would show his feelings, Terence remained silent and concentrated on his driving. Even this early, enough traffic surrounded them to require his attention. Others evidently had also chosen to take advantage of the lovely day.

Lindsey turned her head toward the backseat. "Don't forget—even the courts of law accept as truth whatever is sworn to by several eye witnesses. People saw God through Jesus. Others through the ages heard Him speak. Those of us who haven't actually seen or heard, can seek Him and receive a witness of the truth in our hearts and souls."

Terence held his breath, wondering how Keppler would reply.

"You're right, of course. It is, however, easier to believe in that which you can see, hear, or touch." He laughed. "How did we get so serious, anyway? This is too grand a day to get into a theological discussion. How long before we get to where we start climbing, Terence?"

"Not for a while." Terence grinned at Lindsey, who raised one eyebrow and shrugged. "There's plenty to see along the way, however. This early in the morning we're likely to find deer out, especially once we get off the freeway and onto the back roads."

His prediction proved accurate. Twice before they actually entered Mount Rainier National Park and several times after, graceful deer stepped from the brush alongside the road. One doe bounded across in front of them, causing Patti to squeal for fear they would hit her. Others simply stopped chewing, observed the station wagon and its occupants, and resumed grazing or daintily walked back into the forest.

"What I'd give for a gun right now," Bart exclaimed.

"It wouldn't do you any good. It isn't hunting season and the deer in the park are protected, anyway," Terence told him.

"I can't imagine shooting such a beautiful creature." Patti sounded disappointed the doctor would make such a remark.

"You eat meat, don't you?"

"Domestic animals, not those from the wild."

"My dear child, there's no difference." He laughed at her. "They're just animals, created to provide food for humans."

"There's a difference," she insisted, to Terence's surprise. Patti treated the doctor with such awe, Terence would have surmised she wouldn't contradict anything he said. She went on. "I don't mind if a hunter uses the meat, the way the native Americans did. But many don't. They kill a deer, take the head and horns, maybe a haunch, and leave the rest to rot. It's wicked."

"I agree. Besides, I can find enough meat right in the supermarket," Lindsey put in. "What does our chaplain have to say?"

He waited to make a right turn into a sun-dappled road. Branches interlaced above them, giving a tunnellike atmosphere. "I'm with you girls. Dad and I've hunted and enjoyed it, but we feel its criminal to do so unless you plan to use the meat. Too many hungry people in the world for that. When I was in—"

"Stop!" Lindsey interrupted.

He slammed on the brakes, accompanied by backseat cries of "What's happening?"

"Something moved at the side of the road. An animal." Lindsey stared out the front window. "See, there it is."

Bart leaned forward, one arm draped over the back of the front seat where Lindsey sat. She promptly scooted forward, as if to see better. Terence grinned. "What is it? A dog?" the doctor wanted to know.

"A fox!" Patti whispered. "Isn't he beautiful?"

Terence felt a thrill go through him. "I've seen many coyotes but not many foxes." He gazed at the bushy-tailed animal. "Look at the protective coloration." The orange-red fox with white biblike fur on throat and front blended into the pile of fallen leaves in which it crouched. The fox's unblinking gray-green gaze never left the station wagon.

"Look at the sharp snout and large, pointed ears," Terence said. "Foxes have fantastic hearing and an incredible sense of smell. Would you believe red foxes can hear a mouse squeak over a hundred feet away?"

For several minutes, fox and humans observed each other. The appearance of a car coming toward the wagon disrupted the scene. In a flash, the lovely creature leaped, whirled, and tore off into the forest at the side of the road.

"They are so fast!" Patti gasped.

"Their speed makes them good hunters." Terence took his foot from the brake. "That and their ability to creep silently."

"Does that mean you hate foxes, Patti?" Bart removed his arm from the front seat and leaned back. Terence saw Lindsey relax back into place, and he grinned again.

&

Two hours later they paused after a hard climb up switchbacks that had left them panting. "Either this trail is new, has grown steeper since the last time I came, or I'm out a lot more out of shape than I realized," Lindsey confessed.

"Same here, but what's waiting for us will be worth it."

Patti said between panting, "I'm not sure if I can make it."

"Of course you can," Terence told her. "Don't look ahead at how far we have to go." He laid one hand on her shoulder and gently turned Patti so she faced the series of switchbacks they had just climbed. "Concentrate on how far we've come."

The others also turned. "I wouldn't have believed it." Bart mopped his sweaty forehead. "That's—it can't be the station wagon! It looks like a toy car."

"There's a sermon in what you just said, Terry." Patti grinned impishly. "The next time I get discouraged and feel I'm not getting anywhere on life's rocky road, I'll remember to turn around and see how far I am from where I started." Her face showed she meant every word and even Bart Keppler didn't comment.

Another half hour of walking and Terence announced they'd stop for lunch just ahead. "There's a certain meadow that offers what I consider one of the most awe-inspiring views in the world," he promised. Step after weary step they followed, Lindsey just behind him, Patti and Dr. Keppler following. The trail emerged from the forest and leveled onto a small plateau at the edge of a meadow that sloped upward toward a stand of dark, guarding trees.

Terence slipped out of his backpack, motioned his party to stop, and breathed a prayer of thankfulness when no one spoke. Stillness matched their surroundings. Never had he seen the mountainside more dramatic. The snowy glaciers and gray rock of majestic Mount Rainier stood etched against a blue, blue sky. The meadow preened itself in yellow, orange, and scarlet dress. Even the grass and ground cover flamed crimson and gold from frosty nights, as though determined to flaunt itself in a last, mad, autumn blaze before fading to nothingness beneath the winter snows. Spruce, alpine fir, and other evergreens proudly raised branches in shades of green.

At first Terence heard nothing but the pounding of his heart, the hard breathing of his companions. Gradually, they quieted, and he tuned in to the sounds and feel of creation: lazy air currents that cooled his hot face and made bushes rustle; the hum of insects; a warbling bird; the swish of falling leaves. Peace entered his heart.

He turned to survey his companions. Patti had chosen to sit and lean back against a downed log that had once been a mighty forest monarch. Her rapt, upturned face and blonde hair captured the sunlight. Terence found himself silently praying she might ever walk in the light. The intensity of his petition shocked him. Why should he feel compelled to silently cry out on Patti's behalf, here in this place of peace and contentment?

Terence shifted his gaze toward Bart Keppler, sitting next to her. He tried to read the closed face, to peer deep inside the inscrutable dark eyes that gave no clue to his present thoughts, no betrayal of his feelings or reaction to the beauty before him. Sneaking admiration filled Terence. He had half expected Bart to complain or ask for special consideration during the climb. Bart did not, even though at times he panted like a fox running from hounds. Though he was hot and disheveled, with twigs in his hair from ducking his tall form beneath overhanging trees, he had merely set his lips and kept going. Had Terence misjudged him?

Saving the best for last, the young chaplain surveyed Lindsey. She had walked a few paces away from the others and stood with her hands behind her. He believed she had forgotten the others' presence. From his position a little to one side, Terence saw exaltation in her face, similar to the expression Patti wore, but more pronounced. He averted his gaze, feeling he had unconsciously intruded on a moment between Lindsey and her God.

He could not help looking again. Kinship he seldom felt with anyone except Dad sprang full blown within him when a single diamond drop hovered on her long lashes. How often he had experienced the same sense of wonder.

Did Lindsey feel his regard? Perhaps, for she slowly turned her head and gazed into his face. Terence trembled. Would she resent his intensity? Awareness crept into her watching eyes but no condemnation followed. Rather, he saw the bewildered look of an awakening soul that does not fully understand what has pierced its tranquillity.

He involuntarily took one step toward her. An amused voice stopped him.

"Wonderful as this is, I must admit hunger pangs are rapidly depreciating my ability to admire the flora and fauna." Dr. Keppler laughed ruefully. "You were right, Terence. Memory of breakfast has vanished like a zephyr."

His remarks, although spoken in pleasant tones, clanged in Terence's ears like a cymbal. Was the acting director totally insensitive to the feelings of others? A gleam in the doctor's eyes roused suspicion. Was it just the opposite? While Terence had been watching Lindsey, Keppler could well have been observing both of them and decided to break in. *Don't get paranoid,* Terence told himself. His irrepressible sense of humor came to his rescue. *Maybe the guy's just a jerk. Or hungry, the way he said.*

Terence threw down a plastic tarp from his backpack and they sat cross-legged in a circle, the bounteous lunch in the middle. If Bart had designs on a certain redheaded surgical nurse, he didn't let them show. He kept up a rapid-fire line of questions about Shepherd of Love Hospital that triggered a lively discussion. "I need to learn everything I can before instituting changes," he said frankly.

"What kind of changes?" Patti asked, waving a drumstick like a baton. "We like things the way we are."

"Oh, there's always room for improvement. For instance, is it necessary to require staff members to attend the prayer services before each shift? Don't get me wrong," he hastily added. I'm just wondering if we wouldn't attract a lot of excellent staff members—in addition to those we already have—" He nodded at each of them. "If they could choose whether to attend. After all, a person's religion should be his or her own, not subject to direction in order to hold a job."

"The whole concept of Shepherd of Love, as I understand it, is to combine medical skills with spiritual support," Terence put in. "Isn't this right?"

Patti nodded and Lindsey soberly said, "It's what makes us different from other hospitals. Hiring only Christians is one of the foundations on which the hospital is built." A niggling worry crept into her eyes.

"Yet there are many other sincere persons who could complement our staff," Bart pointed out. "I'm speaking as something of an outsider, of course, but isn't there a danger of the hospital becoming ingrown, or intolerant of others who believe differently?"

"No one forces patients to accept Christianity," Patti protested. She dropped the drumstick and wiped her fingers on a napkin Shane O'Shea had thoughtfully provided. "No one makes them come or stay in Shepherd of Love, either." She stared reproachfully at Dr. Keppler.

He backtracked. "I'm sure I didn't mean to criticize." He bowed his head and when he glanced up he looked chastened. "I just want to do my very best to give the hospital what I believe it most deserves."

Terence couldn't determine whether Bart's expression was reminiscent of Uriah Heep—or whether the look of contrition stemmed from true humility. He forced himself to say, "That's what we all want. Now, who wants to do what?"

"I ate so much lunch, I need to climb some more." Bart stood and smiled his charming smile. "Which of you two young ladies is going with me? Terence, how about you?"

"I'll go." Patti jumped up, eager as a puppy waiting to be petted.

"Lindsey?" A curious glint came to his eyes.

"Thanks, but after last night in Surgery, all this fresh air, sunlight, and good food, I think I'll just sit on the tarp and use the log for a backrest."

"I'll stay and protect her from marauding bears," Terence said.

"Good heavens, there's no danger of that, is there?" Bart looked alarmed.

"Stay on the trail and you shouldn't have a problem." Terence glanced at his watch. "Don't be gone much more than an hour. We have a long hike down and it gets dark earlier than you might think, especially in the forest."

"Okay, boss." Bart saluted smartly and brought his heels together in a quick snap. "Anything else?"

Terence couldn't help laughing at the tomfoolery. "Holler if you need us."

Bart sent a laughing glance toward Lindsey, then said, "Come on, Patti." Swinging hands, they started across the meadow and up the sloping hillside.

"He's a curious combination, isn't he?" Lindsey's statement so paralleled Terence's, he hesitated and she quickly added, "I shouldn't have said that. Forget it, please. How are your chaplain's duties going?" She stretched out on one side of the tarp, arms behind her head to pillow them against the log.

He began to tell her, but before long the elements she'd mentioned earlier did their work well. Lindsey's eyelids closed, fluttered, closed again. Terence smiled. She needed the rest. For a long time he savored the day, then his own short night caught up with him and he too fell asleep.

seven

Lindsey slowly opened her eyes. Terence O'Shea sat slumped against the far end of the fallen log, mahogany hair rumpled and face as innocent as that of a sleeping child. The sight brought a smile to Lindsey's lips. The young chaplain didn't set her heart to fluttering, but she felt good knowing she had such a friend.

For a few moments she remained still, remembering the look that passed between them earlier. Warmth stole into her face and her breath came a little quicker. She had seen something more than friendship in Terry's eyes.

Wide awake now, her nerves twanged. Something felt wrong. She cocked her head and listened. Nothing. Not even the sound of a bird. Where were Bart and Patti? She looked up, noted how low the sun had fallen in the rosy sky, and checked her watch. Alarm filled her.

A full two hours had gone by since Patti and Bart left.

She crawled to the other end of the log. "Terry, wake up! Patti and Bart haven't come back."

He opened sleepy eyes, yawned, and peered into the sky. "Good grief, what time is it?" He sat up and rubbed his eyes.

"More than an hour since you told them to be back. Something must have happened." She reached for the sweatshirt she'd tossed aside earlier in the day. Its fleecy warmth felt good to skin cooled by the dying day. If only she had a fleece to warm her heart.

The last of sleep fled from Terry's eyes and he hastily stood. "Come on. We'll go find them." Lindsey saw the way he glanced at the sun, perched like a giant red pompom on the crest of a distant ridge. Apprehension grayed his eyes, but he smiled at her. "They probably just aren't paying

70

attention to the time. Remember, Keppler's a newcomer to this area."

Patti isn't. The unspoken words hung in the rapidly chilling air. Terence reached down a hand and Lindsey sprang to her feet. "At least we have plenty of food." Her voice sounded loud in the stillness, but thank goodness it didn't tremble. She wished she'd kept still, though; no need to remind Terence of his laughing statement earlier about being well fed in the unlikely event they got caught outside longer than they'd planned.

Terence sharply told her, "We aren't staying out overnight. We're going to locate the others and hightail it out of here as fast as we can. We should have enough time. Besides, Dad would never make up a pack without including a flashlight—and matches, of course." He dug in the backpack and triumphantly waved both items, then snatched up his sweatshirt along with the sweatshirts that belonged to the other two.

"We can't very well start a forest fire just to let people know we're here," Lindsey told him. She laughed in spite of herself and rejoiced when an answering smile curved Terence's lips.

"Ready?" he asked.

"Ready." Following just behind him, she swung into the trail that led through the meadow and grew into a slope. Bart and Patti had trampled down the tall grass and weeds on their climb, so the two searchers made good time. When they reached the top of the nearest rise, Terence cupped his hands around his mouth and shouted, "Bart. Patti."

Bart. Patti. The hills took up the cry. It echoed in the forest and valley below.

Lindsey joined her voice with his. On the third try, they got a response. Far above a faint call of "Here" floated downward to where they stood.

"Are you all right?" Lindsey screamed.

All right. First an echo, then a human cry.

Lindsey sagged with relief. Terence bounded upward. She scrambled after him but had to stop for rest. "Don't wait for me," she pleaded.

He gave her a measuring glance. "Sure you'll be all right?"

"Of course." She panted like a dog, something her father had taught her the very first time the family went for a long hike.

"Back soon," he promised and went on.

She watched him until the path beaten by the other two turned and he vanished from sight. When she had caught her breath, she hurried after him; ears made keen by concern caught Terence's intermittent shouts and their responses. They sounded much nearer now. "Thank You, God." Her strangled prayer came out sounding more like a sob and she quickened her pace.

Ten minutes later, Lindsey again stood on a small, level plateau between two folds of the hills. She gulped in breaths of air and prepared for another climb. Each hill got steeper than the one before. She would need all her energy to forge ahead. How had Bart and Patti managed these steep hills? "They had a lot longer to do it," she muttered. Setting her lips into a firm line that boded no good for the tardy members of the party, she squinted upward. Two gigantic rocks marked the crest of the next rise. Lindsey cast an imploring glance at the reluctant sun hanging onto the remnants of day, then fixed her gaze on the rocks and stepped forward.

The muscles in her legs tightened from exertion. She ignored them and went on, hoping by the time she reached the rocks the others would also be there. A quarter of the way up. Halfway. Three-quarters. She straightened, rubbed her aching leg muscles, and stretched her arms to relieve the cramp in her shoulders.

How still it was! She could be a million miles from another human being. Even though she knew better, the thought plagued her, and she took a step forward.

An awful groaning sound, as if the world felt pain too harsh to bear silently, screeched in her ears. The ground on which she stood shook. Every warning about the massive earthquake seismologists insisted would hit Seattle and the Cascades flashed into Lindsey's mind, faster than the speed of sound. The Big One—and she and her friends were caught in a place as dangerous as downtown Seattle would be should the skyscrapers begin to sway! The noise and shaking continued for what felt like hours but could only be milliseconds. "Please, God, no!" Paralyzing horror gave way to rigid training in how to cope with emergencies.

In one frenzied leap, Lindsey instinctively vaulted to the side of the path and wrapped her arms around a sturdy tree trunk. She burrowed into the needle-covered ground as best she could and buried her face in her arms. A fusillade of debris assaulted her body. Numb and unable to think, she clung to her frail shield against nature and waited.

The rumble became a roar. A mighty wind battered Lindsey's eardrums with its thunder. She felt the breath of it fan her exposed hands, stir her hair. An explosion so loud it forced a scream from her constricted throat told her death stood at her shoulder. She rocked from its impact, hands locked around the tree, knowing only a brief time lay between her and final destruction.

The noise lessened. Stopped. Afraid to move, Lindsey lay motionless. A minute. Two. She raised her head and experimentally twisted her neck. Nothing broken. She opened her eyes to meet a sympathetic ray of sunlight's gleam. Her dazed senses adjusted. The earthquake had passed.

Lindsey unclamped her hands, found them covered with oozing pitch, and literally tore them free. Ecstasy at simply being alive filled her, followed by the sickening knowledge the others might not have fared so well.

"Lindsey?"

The sound of her name overwhelmed her with relief. She tried to call out and discovered her mouth was filled with needles and dirt. She spit them out and managed a feeble, "Here."

Two strong arms circled her half-reclining body. "Thank God!"

"Don't move her," a sharp voice ordered. "She has to be checked for injuries."

For some absurd reason, Lindsey wanted to cry when the security of that pair of arms fell away. "I'm all right." She rolled over and looked first into Terence's chalky face, then Bart Keppler's. "Patti?" A fresh wave of fear surged through her. "Where is she?"

"I'm here," a weak voice whispered. A wet drop splashed on Lindsey's upturned face. "Oh, Lindsey, can you ever forgive me? You could have been killed and it would have been my fault!" A shower followed.

"If you don't stop bawling all over me, I'm going to die by drowning," Lindsey crossly said. "Let me up, will you?" Aware she must be a total mess, she brushed them aside. "For goodness sake, stop crying, Patti. You may be responsible for a lot of things, but causing an earthquake isn't one of them."

Relief softened her voice. "I-I thought you were all dead."

"Dead?" "Earthquake?" "What are you talking about?"

Thoroughly disgusted, Lindsey glared at the three astonished faces. "What's wrong with you all? The Big One that's been predicted for decades comes and you act like you never heard the word earthquake?"

"There was no earthquake, Lindsey." Patti's mouth quivered above her trembling chin.

"Have you gone daft?" she gasped. "No earthquake! What do you call that little performance a few minutes ago?"

Terence lifted her to her feet. Not a trace of blue showed in his eyes. He gently turned her and pointed. "Down there."

She stared at him suspiciously, then shifted her gaze to a canyon far below. An enormous boulder lay amidst the wreckage of shattered small trees and an upheaval of earth.

Dust still rose from where it landed. Lindsey whirled, looked above her. Only one prehistoric-looking stone rested where two had been just a few minutes earlier. The sight made her dizzy, and she clutched at Terence's arm for support. "I don't understand."

"Something caused it to fall. You were directly in its path." His nostrils quivered; the skin across his cheekbones looked tight-drawn, as if he were holding in deep emotion. "Bart, Patti, and I met beyond the first bend on the other side of the crest." He passed a hand over his face as if to blot out the shadow of memory.

"We saw the stone begin to move," Bart explained through bloodless lips. "We ran toward it but could do nothing. When I saw you were in its path, I—"

"Thank God you leaped out of the way," Terence said in a voice so hoarse Lindsey had trouble catching his words.

"If Bart and I hadn't gone so far, it wouldn't have happened," Patti brokenly said. More tears spilled and she flung her arms around Lindsey.

"I don't understand. Why would the boulder suddenly dislodge and hurl itself down the mountain?" Lindsey puzzled. "I've been here before, although not for some time. I've even sat on those stones. They were always sturdy as the Rock of Gibraltar."

"Erosion, perhaps, or the ground may have been softened by rain or snow." Bart's pallor didn't lift. "Terence, if Lindsey isn't hurt, hadn't we better go?" Lindsey's gaze followed his to the ever-lowering sun.

"Yes. If we hurry, we should just about make it. It won't take nearly as long going down as coming up." He led the way back to the lunch site. In short order, they silently folded the tarp, made sure they'd left no trash, and set out single-file in the order they came.

Not for anything would Lindsey admit how shaken she had been. "And it isn't all from the fall," she whispered to herself, so low no one could hear. "God, why did that rock really fall?" Suspicion reared its ugly head. "It-it couldn't have been loosened, could it?" An ice-water chill poured down her back and made her shudder. "If so, who?"

Patti? To believe she had either cause or physical strength to undermine a boulder—if it had been undermined—in hopes of killing her best friend was the worst kind of insanity.

Bart Keppler? What reason would Bart have for attempting to kill the nurse he obviously admired? Unless he were psychotic, the fact Lindsey had rejected his advances wouldn't trigger such a horrible act. Nothing in his demeanor hinted at mental instability. Besides, he wouldn't have had opportunity, unless he and Patti had been apart during the time they absented themselves from camp. How could she find out if they had separated for a time, especially, near the rocks? Unless approached in the exact right way, Patti would be furious; in spite of her concern for Lindsey, Patti's eyes betrayed that the afternoon had strengthened her growing attraction for Dr. Keppler. She might also let slip her roommate's probing and alert the acting director.

Terence? Lindsey grinned at the thought of evil lurking behind his open face. On the other hand, of the three above her on the mountain, the young chaplain would have been the only one alone at the rocks. His comment rang in her brain. "Bart, Patti, and I met beyond the first bend on the other side of the crest." How far ahead of the last member of the party had he actually been? Would he have had time to dig around the boulder? He also was the only one of the three who knew Lindsey came along behind him.

A terrible thought occurred to Lindsey just as the weary party started down the last switchback. If the boulder had been loosened with murderous intent, only two answers were valid: either Terence wanted to kill a certain redheaded surgical nurse, or he was the intended target, set up by Bart Keppler for some obscure reason.

Horror filled her. She choked back a cry of protest. Satan

himself must be filling her heart and mind with his poison for her to allow these ghastly thoughts to linger. Killer or victim. Killer or victim. The words beat time to her footsteps, even though she tried to crowd them out. Intent on her battle with fear, guilt, and fatigue, she stumbled and slid a bit on the needle-covered ground before recovering herself.

"All right, Lindsey?" Terence stopped and turned toward her. Only a little light remained. Soon they would have to rely on the flashlight.

The steadiness in his eyes reassured her. She hadn't realized how deeply her doubts had entrenched themselves until she met Terry's gaze. "I'm all right."

"Good. It isn't far now. Patti, Bart, are you making it okay?"

"Uh huh." Patti wiped her face with a tissue. "You don't happen to have some of those leftover turnovers handy enough to reach, do you?" She sounded so wistful the other three chortled, but Terence slipped the backpack off and rummaged in it.

"Patricia Thompson, you are the limit," Lindsey told her. "Can't you wait until we get to the bottom?"

"I suppose so. I just thought we could use the extra energy." Patti was obviously regaining her usual aplomb. She squealed with delight when Terry handed her a turnover. "Mmm. Even better than at lunch."

"Bart? Lindsey?"

"Sure." Keppler took the offering, but Lindsey shook her head.

"My hands are all pitchy." She hadn't realized until now how hungry she'd grown on the long hike down.

"I'll tip back the edge of the plastic wrapping and you can eat it like a taco in a napkin," Terence told her. She couldn't remember anything tasting better.

They stopped at a gas station on the way home. The understanding owner obligingly lent her a cleaner, "guaranteed to take everything off but the skin." She came from the women's room with hands spotless, although shriveled from scrubbing.

"Do you want to stop for dinner?" Terence asked.

Lindsey surveyed her filthy, disheveled clothing. "If you don't mind, I'd rather just polish off the picnic lunch and get home to a warm tub."

"I second the motion." Bart Keppler's strong, supporting voice mingled with Patti's, "Me, too—especially if there's another turnover."

"There is." Terence pulled the station wagon into a well-lighted spot not far from the gas station. "Let me see if they have hot coffee. We can use it." He walked back toward the station, cheerfully whistling, and returned with a large thermos and four thermal cups.

The liquid warmed Lindsey from the soles of her sturdily-shod feet to the crown of her filthy head. She'd combed out what debris she could in the light of the rest room mirror, but she needed a good shampoo. Once they finished the last delicious crumb, she felt sleep encroaching on her eyelids. "Will your father worry?" she mumbled.

"I called him from the station."

Terence's voice sounded like it came from a far distance. She vaguely heard Patti's soft laugh and Bart's low voice. They faded. The next thing she knew, something prodded her shoulder, and Patti ordered, "Wake up, Sleeping Beauty. We're home."

Somehow she stumbled from the station wagon. "Ugh. Every bone in my body hurts. I feel as if I slid down the mountain along with that boulder." She regretted her remark the minute it popped out. The last thing she needed was to start thinking morbid thoughts and lie awake half the night trying to solve a crime that probably had never been committed.

Dr. Keppler gallantly walked Patti to the apartment door, after a veiled glance at Lindsey, who followed with Terence.

For some reason, the chaplain dawdled. His stride so little resembled his usual ground-covering pace that Lindsey wondered, *Does he have a reason? Or does he just want to give Bart the chance to kiss Patti good night?*

On impulse, she stopped, stood on tiptoe, and whispered, "Why do you think that boulder toppled and fell?"

"I don't know and there's no way to find out." He looked somber. "Perhaps it's as Keppler said. Erosion, or soft earth from rain."

"Do you really believe that?" she demanded.

"There's no reason to suspect it happened any other way." Terence faced her squarely. "I can't think of justification to believe it more than a freak accident but—" His harsh voice sent shivers through her and he gripped her fingers until they hurt. "One thing, Lindsey. Patti and Bart are sure to mention what happened, but keep your questions to yourself. Don't mention them to anyone. Understand? Not to anyone."

He dropped her hand, turned on his heel, and walked away, a grim man, far removed from the whistling hospital chaplain whose familiar grin automatically brought cheer.

eight

Killer or victim.

The words pounded in Lindsey's imagination through a long soak in the tub and far into the night, like a metronome set to eternally tick out its measured beat. What had Terence O'Shea meant by his cryptic warning? Lindsey's mind ran double track. If innocent, but suspicious, he'd certainly be concerned for her safety. If guilty, he would definitely want her to keep silent.

"He can't be a murderer," she protested into her pillow, body rigid as a soldier as attention. "Not with those eyes and that innocent face."

Not necessarily true, a little voice inside argued. You've seen victims who trusted in persons with innocent faces that hid souls filled with evil.

Killer or victim.

Dr. Keppler? "He couldn't have tried to kill me," Lindsey wearily whispered. She remembered the shock in his face, and a spark of hope touched her for a moment. The next instant an unpleasant truth hit her with battering ram force and suspicion flamed again.

Dr. Keppler's shock could have been to find her alive.

Or from learning the boulder had almost killed the wrong person.

Lindsey threw back her blankets and ran noiselessly to the bathroom, afraid she'd be sick. The faces of the two men danced before her: both new to Shepherd of Love Hospital; both Christians—or so it appeared. Did one of those faces hide slimy depths, an unseen motive strong enough to justify murder? If so, which one?

Her system revolted, but long, deep breaths followed by

splashes of cold tap water to her face returned her stomach to normal. Clinging to a forlorn hope, she gazed into the bathroom mirror without seeing the troubled reflection staring back. Perhaps the whole thing had been from natural causes. If so, she was doing both men a grave injustice by harboring unfounded suspicion. She clutched the idea like drowning persons clutch anything that will support them until they reach safety

Lindsey reluctantly took a mild sedative from the medicine cabinet, hating the need for it but knowing she needed sleep to clear her mind. "Things always seem hopeless in the middle of the night," she whispered. A faint grin at the Best family maxim brightened her mood. She followed with the rest of it, "And they always get better in the morning light." She tiptoed to the kitchen on silent, nurse's feet and warmed a glass of milk. Usually that alone relaxed her. Tonight, the addition of the sedative sent her into a deep, restful sleep, the best healing possible for her tired body and battered mind.

A bright September morning proved the second part of the Best saying right. It seemed incredible anyone would want to harm either Terence or her. With a light heart, she chattered on the way to breakfast with Patti and Shina. Yet when the blonde nurse regaled those at the table with the story of Lindsey's near-escape, a blanket of depression fell over her again and she hastily rose. "Since I was there during the gruesome details, I'm sure you can spare me." She tempered the remark with a grin, hoping her voice didn't sound as thin to them as it did her.

Patti was too engrossed in the story to notice, but Lindsey saw Shina's quick look of dismay. Lindsey managed a smile, waved, and headed out of the dining room, glad to be off until the next day. The climbing, not to mention the strain of hanging on to the tree trunk while the world disintegrated around her, had taken a far greater toll than she'd realized until now. Maybe she should go back to bed. She shook her head emphatically. No. She'd only lie there and rehash yesterday.

Lindsey considered her options. Shepherd of Love attempted to schedule personnel so most could attend services in the Chapel or a church of their choice. However, in the weeks since the new chaplain came, Lindsey had either been unable to get away or had gone home over Sunday. Should she go to Chapel services or the nearby church she and her friends sometimes attended? She privately admitted to reluctance, a desire for more time before seeing Terence again. She must not let him know she secretly carried doubts about him. His blue eyes would darken to angry gray, the way they had yesterday when he found her pitchy and dirt-covered beside the trail.

Lindsey stopped short. *Don't be a ninny*, she ordered herself. *The best way in the world to establish his innocence or guilt is to go hear him preach.*

Lindsey unhurriedly walked back to her apartment, sunlight warm as a benediction on her head and arms. She turned her face toward Mount Rainier, dreading the moment for fear its snow-capped visage would repel her. She loved the mountain and had looked east every day as far back as she could remember. As she gazed at it she remembered her father's laughing comment, "In California, the cry is, 'surf's up.' In Seattle, it's 'mountain's out.'" She smiled, and her heart filled with relief. Yesterday's horror did not have the power to spoil the grandeur for her, the sense of awe at this particular facet of God's creation.

She remembered how her father had changed from joking to seriousness, the look of wonder in his face when he quoted from Psalms 121: "I will lift up mine eyes unto the hills, from whence cometh my help. My help cometh from the Lord, which made heaven and earth. He will not suffer thy foot to be moved; he that keepeth thee will not slumber."

Lindsey drew in a ragged breath. God certainly had not

been slumbering when she needed help on that mountain trail. He had kept her safe from the worst danger she'd ever encountered. She bowed her head. Her heart swelled with thankfulness too deep for words, yet she knew He heard.

The song of a robin roused her from her reverie and she lightly ran inside. Time to change for worship. Fifteen minutes later, Lindsey surveyed her pale-green-clad self. Fall might be here, but her heart felt more like spring and she had dressed accordingly. She touched a light, flowerlike cologne to wrists and behind her ears, slid her feet into plain white pumps, and reached for her worn Bible, a gift from her father on her seventeenth birthday. Normally, gifts came from both parents, but Ramsey Best had broken tradition that year.

"We're going on a shopping trip," he told his daughter. If she lived to be a hundred, she'd never forget it. Although all family members had Bibles, they were of necessity inexpensive editions. Lindsey had thrilled when her father took her to the largest Christian bookstore in the city and told her to pick out any Bible she wanted. She felt like a child set free in a candy store. Her father reminded her they had all the time they needed, so she browsed to her heart's content.

At last she selected a soft, clear print King James Version. "Lindsey Best" in gold letters adorned the black leather cover, and she seldom used another Bible.

"Mom and Dad taught us stories from the King James Version. I'm used to it," she explained when friends pointed out advantages of The Living Bible, The New International Version, and others. "Besides, I like the poetic rhythm of the traditional language."

Now she hugged the Book to her, caught up a white purse, and headed for the Chapel, wondering what Terence would choose for his morning text. Hospital gossip had it he preached like an old-time revivalist, head thrown back, fearless in his proclamations.

Patti didn't make it to the worship service, but Dr. Keppler was already there when Lindsey arrived. She chose a seat across the aisle and back a row. It gave her a good view of his handsome profile. She examined his face carefully and heaved a sigh of relief. Not a trace of villain showed. Shina—charming in an apricot-colored pants uniform—slid in beside Lindsey during the rousing hymn, "All Hail the Power of Jesus' Name." Her clear soprano blended beautifully with Lindsey's alto and added harmony. The chaplain led the song in a resonant voice that made Lindsey think of mighty armies marching for God. She took a deep breath. Much as she loved the former chaplain, Terry O'Shea's approach blew through the Chapel like a salty ocean breeze, changing worship from quiet meditation to active participation. Yet an underlying current of reverence shone in the young minister's face.

His sermon kept the nurses and other worshippers on the edge of their seats from the time he quoted in a voice filled with conviction Paul's crystal-clear statement, "For all have sinned, and come short of the glory of God"(Romans 3:23). Terence neither ranted nor raved. He did not pound the desk or wave his arms. Instead, he left the platform, stepped to the middle of the center aisle, and talked to his flock, a shepherd called to minister. His open Bible lay in one hand.

"We hear a lot these days how God is unconditional love. This is true. We also hear Jesus accepts us just as we are. Wrong." His voice rang in the stillness of complete attention. "I believe this is the most dangerous teaching ever to come forth in the history of Christianity, an insidious doctrine fostered by Satan to deceive the world and God's children."

A murmur of surprise rippled through the listeners. Lindsey's mouth dropped open. She shot a surreptitious glance toward Bart Keppler. He sat with arms crossed, one dark eyebrow raised. In scorn? Skepticism? Lindsey tore her gaze free and concentrated on the sermon.

"Jesus loves us as we are. He died that we might live. But He cannot accept us as we are. To do so would negate everything He taught." He held up his Bible. "Each recorded incident concerning someone who met the Master face to face ends with a command to go forth and become a new person. Christ's message was simple, 'Go and sin no more.'"

Lindsey looked around her. A few people nodded. Some faces showed understanding. Others looked stunned. A muscle twitched in Bart Keppler's cheek, the only movement in his curiously still body.

Lindsey sat spellbound. Some of what Terence said reflected things she had pondered. The fine line between tolerance and permissiveness. The courage to take an unpopular stand among friends away from the hospital. She leaned forward, eager to hear every word.

Terence held his hands out, palms upward. "We cannot choose for others, but God help us if we do not make sure they know where we stand, and why." His face grew shadowed. "Never condemn a person, only those actions the Lord abhors. Learn to disagree without being disagreeable. In so doing, the Holy Spirit will guide you in what you say. The same Spirit can put a check on your lips and teach you when to be still."

He paused and the blue of Puget Sound on the brightest day filled his eyes when he looked from face to face. "The single most important thing you can do is this: be a living example, a sermon in flesh, blood, and bones."

Lindsey fancied his gaze lingered on Bart Keppler's face a little longer than the rest, and she chided herself for what might be fancy. She met Terence's steady gaze when it rested on her, and she wondered what he would make of the relief she could not conceal. No man could preach as Terry O'Shea had done and still be a menace, unless he were the biggest hypocrite who ever lived. That she could not believe.

The remainder of the service took on a dream-like quality. Shina slipped out during the final hymn to go back on duty. Terence ended the worship, "May the peace of God be with you all, now and forever. Amen."

Lindsey got out of the Chapel and part way down the corridor before Bart Keppler caught up with her. Her heart bounced out of all proportion to his commonplace question, "Feeling all right? I was surprised to see you here this morning."

She found herself unwillingly responding to his smile. "I'm fine." She paused in mid-stride, the eagerness in his dark eyes sounding off a warning bell in her brain. "At least so far. I'll probably take the rest of the day to laze around."

His smile vanished. "Too bad. I hoped you'd spend it with me." A curious glint showed that whatever he had done the day before to make Patti look so radiant didn't exclude his desire to date her roommate.

"I just wouldn't be good company," Lindsey said.

"Is that an excuse?" he wanted to know. "I thought you had a good time at the Space Needle with me."

Lindsey debated. Should she evade the question she felt would lead to a confrontation? If so, it would mean trying to avoid him and making herself look ridiculous in the process.

"Well?" His voice crackled like splintering crystal.

She looked straight into Bart's eyes and saw a flicker of actual dislike. With sudden clarity, she knew whatever reason he had for trying to date her didn't involve caring. Ego, maybe, or pride, but not actual admiration. It made her unpleasant task easier. "I don't intend to lose my best friend in order to date you, Dr. Keppler," she told him pointblank.

"Bart," he automatically corrected. "Suppose I tell you Patti means nothing to me, that I only dated her to learn more about you?"

The invincible male, Lindsey thought. Refusing to admit a female existed who didn't bow to his charm. The thought steadied her. She decided to see if he'd allow her to play it light. Mischief ran from her toes to her face and she deliberately twinkled her eyes, knowing they reflected the green of her dress. "I'd say you're a real con artist—"

Her plan backfired. Bart turned pale, grabbed her arm, and hissed, "Just what is that supposed to mean?"

She wrenched free and rubbed the red marks his fingers left. "My word, but you're jumpy! Don't you recognize the light touch when you hear it? If you had let me finish, I'd have said when it comes to flirting."

Color returned to his face. "Sorry. It's just that I really do like you."

Again she desperately tried to lighten the atmosphere. "In the words of the man whose wife told him he couldn't expect everyone to like him, 'what's not to like?'" It sounded fatuous in her ears but served to bring a half-smile to his lips. Lindsey pressed her advantage. "I'd better get to the dining room."

"May I come with you?" He sounded uncharacteristically humble.

"Of course." Her lips twitched. Once after an influx of too many relatives who stayed entirely too long in the crowded Best home, one of Lindsey's brothers whispered, "Know what hospitality is? The art of making people feel at home when you wish they were." Now she knew exactly what he meant.

Patti and Shina were already at a table. The blonde nurse's eyes lit up when they entered and Lindsey's heart plunged. Why must her friend be vulnerable to this false-hearted man who would carelessly dismiss her in favor of dating someone for whom he cared nothing? Didn't it point to a darker, more devious side than the smiling hospital director showed to the world at large?

"Room for one more?" Terence's cheerful voice broke into her brown study.

"Sure." She scooted closer to Shina, making space next to Bart, who promptly scowled and bent a black look toward her. After she assuaged the first pangs of hunger, she laid down her fork and remarked, "I appreciated your sermon."

"Thanks."

"So did I," Shina put in. "It made me realize my timidity in speaking out."

"Imposing your beliefs on someone else, you mean?" Dr. Keppler had evidently decided to play devil's advocate.

"Is that what you got out of my sermon?" Terence inquired.

Bart shrugged. "Pretty much. I've always felt it would be arrogant of me to be so sure I am right about something I can tell the world how to live. Isn't that why God gave people agency? Who's to say only one way is the right way?"

"Isn't that strange talk for a Christian?" Terry quietly asked.

Bart looked startled, even a little alarmed. "Of course not. It's like traveling to New York. We can choose to fly, take a train, or drive." His smile reminded Lindsey of a white reef on a night-darkened shore. "We can even walk or ride horseback. It may take us longer to get there, but the destination's the same."

Patti looked thoughtful, but Shina objected, "Some may get sidetracked and never get there at all."

"Sorry, Shina, that's a stock answer."

He sounded so patronizing Lindsey wanted to hit him. To her amazement, Shina didn't back down as she expected her friend to do. She quietly replied, "So is your example."

Terence had a sudden coughing fit and buried his face in a napkin. Patti looked distressed. Lindsey bit back a laugh at the look on Bart's face. To her amazement, he laughed. "Touché. You're a worthy opponent, Miss Ito. Or should I make that Ms.?"

"Shina will do," she pertly told him.

He laughed again and rose. "See you later, everyone." He sauntered out with head high, not at all like one beaten at his own game by a nurse half his size.

"Why do you all pick on him?" Patti cried when he had

gone, keeping her voice low enough so those around couldn't hear. "Bart's doing a wonderful job here. Everyone says so. Why don't you like him?"

Lindsey frantically searched her heart and said honestly, "There are a lot of things about Dr. Keppler to admire. It's just that some of his ideas are odd."

"They aren't odd at all." Patti's eyes flashed blue fire. "He explained to me yesterday his dream is for all the world to live in peace and he will do everything he can to make it happen."

A squiggle of disbelief played tag up and down Lindsey's spine. If Dr. Bart Keppler were so intent on peace, why did he keep trying to make trouble between two of the hospital's longest-term nurses and best friends?

nine

The empty warehouse repelled the dark figure, who had learned to loathe it. With winter coming on, there had to be a better contact place. When the phone finally rang, his irritation showed in the barked, "Yes?"

"Well?"

"The problem is a lot more serious than I thought."

Ominous silence, then, "What are you going to do about it?"

"I don't know. Why can't we try elsewhere?"

"You fool! This is a prototype. If we pull off here what we must, the whole world will know and applaud. Others are prepared and waiting, ready to follow our lead. Here's what you're to do." A long list of instructions followed, ending with, "Strike now, I tell you, or take the consequences." The click of the disconnected call rang like a distant knell in the listener's ear.

Five minutes later a huddled figure slipped unobserved from the warehouse. It all sounded so simple, yet had the brain planning the operation failed to take in one crucial thing: the human factor? The success or failure of the whole project rested on raggedly clad shoulders. Not just the project, but the future direction of the world. A furtive glance into the brutish night did nothing to dispel his gloom. On dispirited feet, the figure melted into the night, burdened by the part he had to play. Had anyone other than God—if there were a God—ever faced such a monumental challenge?

❧

On a dreary November morning, Dr. Keppler caught up with Lindsey just outside the hospital dining room. "I have tickets for Saturday night for the Seattle Opera House," he told her as blandly as if she hadn't consistently refused to go out with him. "Don't say you're on duty. I know you just got transferred to days for the next week."

"I wasn't going to." She gave him a measuring look. "Thank you for the invitation but I told you how I feel."

A flare of dislike marred the beauty of the watching, dark eyes.

Lindsey impulsively laid one hand on his well-tailored sleeve. "I don't mean to make you angry. After all, we have to work together. Please don't embarrass either of us by bringing this up again."

Mockery replaced the anger in his eyes. Bart waited until a group of laughing employees passed them and in a voice calculated to reach her ears alone, he said, "I never get angry. I get even." He closed one hand over hers.

You are furious right now, Lindsey wanted to retort. She snatched her hand away and felt her temper rise. "Just what do you mean by that cryptic remark?"

Laughing innocence banished the last of Dr. Keppler's annoyance. Chameleonlike, he became his usual, suave self. "My, my, Nurse Lindsey, are we so hostile this morning we can't recognize a joke when we hear one?" He glanced out the window at streaming rain. "Must be the weather is getting you down. Three days of downpour is enough to put anyone out of sorts."

His condescending manner infuriated the red-haired nurse. "I meant what I said." Lindsey turned her back on him and walked away, biting her lip to keep from hurling words at him she'd later regret. A piece of long-ago advice from her father steadied her emotions. "A rude comment brands the speaker, not the person to whom it is made," Ramsey Best had said to his tearful daughter after a teasing child poked fun at Lindsey's coppery hair.

Now she clenched her capable hands, wondering how the acting hospital director would like it if those same hands wrung his precious neck. The thought made her lips twitch, and she gave a little skip in the empty corridor.

When she reached the Chapel, the door stood open. She glanced at her watch, noted a little time remained before she had to report to Surgery, and stepped inside. Terence O'Shea sat in the front pew, head bowed, shoulders slumped in either fatigue or discouragement. Strange. No one had said anything at breakfast about losing a patient. What else could bring that droop to the wide shoulders usually squared against the world and its adversities?

Shocked by seeing the young chaplain in an unguarded moment, the watching nurse blinked. A curious tenderness went through her, even though she felt like an intruder. Could she get away before she disturbed him?

Lindsey hadn't counted on the fact that Terence's ears had grow keen from months of light sleeping in case his father needed him in the night. He rose and turned toward her, one hand behind his back. His haggard face little resembled the laughing Terry she knew. An exclamation of dismay escaped her and she hurried forward. "What's wrong? Is it your father?"

"No." The mahogany-red head slowly moved back and forth. "Dad's actually a little better." Not a trace of a smile curved the straight lips.

"Then why—"

Terence wordlessly withdrew his right hand from behind his back, held it out, and unclenched his fingers.

Lindsey recoiled from the object resting on the chaplain's open palm. Her heart leaped to her throat in one giant bound. Her eyes burned. She felt color drain from her face and grabbed the end of a pew to steady herself. She took in great gulps of air. "What—it's not—it can't be—"

"It is." Terry's eyes glazed with shock. "A voodoo doll."

"At Shepherd of Love? Impossible!" Lindsey couldn't tear her fascinated gaze from the ghastly thing. A moment later, a fresh wave of horror assailed her. Her voice came out strangled, disbelieving. "Terry, the doll—it looks like you!"

"Complete with a pin through the heart. I saw this kind of thing in Haiti."

She barely heard him. "Wh-where did you find it?" Her stomach churned and she swallowed hard.

"Someone shoved it under the Bible on the altar."

From sanctuary and peace, the Chapel instantly changed to a place fraught with fear and darkness. Lindsey's teeth chattered. "What does it mean? What shall we do?"

Rage darkened Terry's eyes to gray. He hurled the obscene symbol of evil across the Chapel with all his might. "Don't do anything, Lindsey." He gripped her shoulders and lightly shook her for emphasis. "Until I find out who is responsible for this, the best way to baffle the guilty person is to remain silent." He looked at her appealingly. "I know it's asking a lot, but if you really want to help, go on to work and say nothing. Not to anyone, hear me?"

She nodded, realizing the wisdom of what he said. "I'll try."

His grip relaxed. The beginning of a smile returned blue to his eyes. "You can do it." His forehead wrinkled. "We need to meet. Are you free after work?"

"Yes."

"Good. I'll call for you at six." He considered. "Wear jeans, will you, please? I'd rather not discuss this here at the hospital. You know the warning about walls having ears."

She shuddered. "You can't think anyone from Shepherd of Love is responsible! That's preposterous." Yet even as she disclaimed the possibility, cold reason told her differently. Who had a better chance to plant such a gruesome thing than a member of the hospital staff? Besides, who outside the hospital hated Terence O'Shea enough to send such a bizarre warning?

All day, between patients, Lindsey found the same questions haunting her. Day shift was far different from night, when much of the surgical work was emergency or accident generated. Unexpected things did come up, but for the most part, surgery followed surgery on a more orderly, scheduled basis, with breaks in between. The calm exterior routine gave her interior thoughts the chance to spin in frantic circles.

By six o'clock, Lindsey had showered and donned light blue denims. She slid into a matching shirt enhanced by red, green, and blue embroidered flowers and leaves, then opted for a green head band that brought out the green in her eyes.

Terry's tired face brightened when she opened the apartment door for him. "You look like a farm girl."

"You said to wear jeans. I've been wondering why all day," she confessed.

"They'll allow you to sit on the rug in front of a fireplace and still be comfortable," he teased. "I'll get into mine as soon as we get home."

"Home—oh, you're taking me to meet your father?"

"I called and told him to throw an extra plate on the table. We can talk freely there." He glanced uneasily around the quiet apartment. "Where's Patti?"

"Out with Dr. Keppler." Lindsey didn't describe the ecstatic way her roommate had floated in and announced they were going to Ivar's Salmon House for dinner. *If he truly liked her, I wouldn't care,* Lindsey mentally reasoned. *I don't think he does. I suspect this is simply the opening gun in his get-even campaign.*

❧

"You didn't tell her or Shina—"

Lindsey felt herself tense. "I told no one anything." She shivered. "I'd rather not think about it at all, but we can't just ignore it, can we?"

"No." A worried look crept into his face. "Shall we go?"

Lindsey caught up the warmly lined denim jacket that completed her outfit and followed Terry to the parking lot. Once inside the station wagon and headed away from Seattle, she wistfully asked, "It couldn't be just a childish prank? Someone trying to scare you or the hospital?"

"I wish." His hands tightened on the wheel. The somber note in his voice killed any hope Lindsey had that it was all a bad joke. "The way the voodoo doll was tucked under the Bible makes me think it's a direct and diabolical challenge to God and all He stands for from some occult, Satanic force." He paused. "If it's all right with you, let's wait and discuss it with Dad. He's more level-headed and less hot-headed than his son."

She laughed and some of the gloom vanished. For the rest of the drive, they chatted on lighter subjects. They speculated as to when the hospital director might return, touched on one subject then another.

Never self-conscious, Lindsey found herself eagerly anticipating meeting Shane O'Shea. She'd put together a fairly accurate picture of the older man as much from the love and respect in his son's voice as the vivid vignettes Terence wove of his childhood. "You love the farm, don't you?"

"Yes. With the hospital chaplaincy, I have the best of both worlds." Buoyancy filled his rich voice. "Especially now. One of God's most recent answers to prayer came in the form of a neighbor. He and Dad made an arrangement for him to farm and care for our land on shares. It means we can keep the place and the crops will generate enough interest for taxes and repairs." He laughed. "A chaplain's salary doesn't include owning a place that doesn't pull its own weight."

Shane O'Shea turned out to be everything Lindsey expected and more. His keen blue eyes so like his son's beamed welcome, yet Lindsey felt she'd been thoroughly examined in one lightning glance. The silver in his hair, deeply etched facial lines, and gnarled hands bore mute witness Shane was no stranger to pain, yet in repose, he wore peace like a banner.

Lindsey ate until she felt ashamed. "Mr. O'Shea, even my mother can't make a better pot roast! This is velvety as cheese." She cut another gravy-covered piece with her fork and raised it to her mouth. The accompanying carrots, potatoes, and onions, Shane said, had simmered all afternoon in an old-fashioned Dutch oven. They were followed by wild blackberry dumplings made from fruit grown on the O'Shea land.

Terence insisted on doing the dishes, leaving his father and Lindsey to get acquainted. True to his prediction, she curled up on an old-fashioned hooked rug that lay in front of the fireplace, warmed as much by Shane's personality as the merry little orange and red flames before her. He sat in a nearby recliner, a lap robe over his outstretched feet and legs. By the time Terence joined them, Lindsey felt she'd known his father forever.

"May I bring my family here someday?" she asked. "They'd love it." *And you,* she added to herself.

"Of course. Any or all of them." Shane smiled at her. "They sound like our kind of people."

She realized he had learned a great deal about her from the few simple questions he'd asked.

Shane turned to Terence, who had dropped to the rug next to Lindsey and sat cross-legged beside her. "All right, son. What's the trouble?"

Lindsey gasped. "Are you by any chance psychic?"

"No, lass. I just know my boy and something is amiss."

She tucked the comment away to take out and dissect later, then inhaled sharply when Terence held up the grotesque voodoo doll he'd thrown aside so violently earlier that day.

Shane reared back in his chair and bellowed, "For the love of Mike, is that what I think it is?" The peace in his face fled before the same turmoil Lindsey had experienced hours before.

"Yes, it is, Dad." Terry laid it in his father's lap. "I found it today in the Chapel."

"I wouldn't have believed it. Not in Shepherd of Love." Shane fixed his piercing blue gaze on his son. Lindsey had the feeling he had forgotten her presence. "Did you make enemies in Haiti?"

Terence looked surprised. "Of course. We weren't at all popular with the witch doctors, especially—"

Lindsey couldn't hold back her curiosity. "What on earth were you doing in Haiti, trafficking with witch doctors?" She clasped her hands and leaned forward, feeling on the edge of some fantastic mystery. The snapping of wood in the fireplace made a perfect setting for whatever story Terry might tell.

He looked astonished. "I thought I told you." He paused. "Actually, I guess I started to a couple of times and got interrupted. Anyway, I went to Haiti as chaplain on a medical mission ship. Learned enough medicine to help where I could, under supervision, of course. Our simplest antibiotics cured dozens of those who swarmed to us for all kinds of help." His face turned grim in the firelight. "The local witch doctors hated anyone who showed them up. They especially hated me because I offered spiritual as well as physical help whenever I got the chance. A few of the patients actually found the courage to break free from the black magic that's practiced freely in Haiti. Some moved to other areas to avoid being harmed." He broke off and faced Lindsey. "How much do you know about voodoo?"

"Not much." She tried to lighten the heavy mood. "I don't have more than one or two witch doctors among my friends." The shock in Terry's eyes made her ashamed of her levity. So did the involuntary sound of protest from Shane. "I'm sorry. I don't mean to treat this lightly. I guess my brain can't accept such a thing could enter Shepherd of Love."

"The serpent entered Eden," Shane reminded.

"I know," she choked. One hand flew to her throat. "It's just that the hospital stands for everything right and good."

"All the more reason for the forces of evil to attack it." Shane's quiet voice sent ice splinters through Lindsey. She shifted position and hugged her knees to her chest.

"Satan concentrates on persons or institutions that pose a threat. Why should he waste time in areas not engaged in doing good?"

Lindsey hunched closer to the fire, wishing it would melt the rapidly growing glacier in her heart.

"If we're to stamp this out right now before it gets worse, I'll need your help," Terry said frankly. "I haven't been at Shepherd of Love long enough to know who can be trusted and who can't. How about it, Lindsey? Will you be my co-partner in fighting crime?" He laughed. "Maybe we can write a book when we solve our first case and call it *Secret at Shepherd of Love.*"

"Now who's being facetious?" Shane demanded.

"Crime? Do you really expect other incidents?" Lindsey's mind whirled. "I mean, this is only one."

Terence stretched out flat on his back, arms folded beneath his head. "I'm not so sure about that. Someone broke into Personnel, you know. I learned yesterday my file never did turn up."

"Is anyone else's missing?"

He looked disconcerted. "Yes, but it might be a red herring." Terry grimaced. "An amateur detective five minutes and already I'm beginning to sound like a sleuth. Anyway, Dr. Keppler's file is also gone, which makes sense. Personnel was so swamped when we applied, our information didn't get entered into the computer."

"Perhaps your file is the red herring." Shane fitted the fingers of one hand against those of the other. "Without those files, what does the hospital really know about either you or Dr. Keppler, except what you told them?

His direct question left Lindsey gasping. "T.D.M," she muttered.

"Excuse me?" Terry sat up and stared as if she'd gone mad.

Lindsey felt red crawl clear up to her hairline. "Tall, dark, and mysterious. That's what Shina nicknamed Dr. Keppler." She laughed nervously. "I know it's silly and Patti says it's unchristian—which it probably is." The sheer astonishment on the men's faces restored her equilibrium. "Oh, dear, I'm babbling. Besides, it's too silly to mention."

"Nothing can be considered silly that may have a bearing on this," Terry reminded her.

"It's just that Shina took an instant aversion to Dr. Keppler. She said she once read a Western novel with a villain named Black Bart. Every time she saw Dr. Keppler, she thought of it because his name's Bartholomew. I read the book, too."

Terry's shout of laughter cleared the air. "So you read the book, too. What's your impression of our acting director?"

A note of eagerness beneath the seemingly casual question caused Lindsey to consider well before she replied. "I honestly don't know. He can be charming—when he gets his own way." She squirmed, not wanting to go into the details of her stormy relationship with the dark-haired doctor.

"And when he doesn't?" Shane dropped his hands to the voodoo doll in his lap and an unreadable expression crossed his face.

"Sometimes he wears a biding-my-time look. At other times, he mocks. Or shows quickly suppressed anger." She stopped, unable to add more.

"Same impressions I got the day we climbed on Mount Rainier," Terry put in.

A stick snapped in the fireplace, sounding overly loud in the hushed room. Lindsey jumped. Surely God wouldn't let anything destroy the work being done for Him at Shepherd of Love! She glanced at the menacing voodoo doll still in Shane O'Shea's lap. The danger could well be directed toward Terry, not the hospital. A spurt of fear went through her. In order to squelch it, she quickly said, "If I'm going to be your helper, I have to be informed. Tell me about voodoo, please." Yet even as she asked, her inner self longed to flee the feeling of evil that hung over her request like a floating shroud.

ten

Uncertainty crept into Terence O'Shea's face. "Are you sure you want to hear this?" he asked Lindsey, who sat wide-eyed on the rug in front of the fireplace. "It's dark and frightening. Things that go bump in the night don't even come close to the terror that voodoo creates—and not just in its followers."

"Really?" Shane O'Shea glanced down at the voodoo doll that had been made in a crude caricature of his son. With a motion of distaste, he flung it toward the dying flames.

"Don't!" Some instinct beyond herself caused Lindsey to intercept the flying missile in a catch spectacular enough to make even her football playing brothers proud. "Put the horrid thing away. Who knows? We may need it sometime for evidence." She dropped the doll and rubbed her fingers on her jeans, scouring them against the denim until they stung.

"If you'd like to wash your hands, we'll understand," Terry gruffly told her.

"I would." A good scrubbing in the large farmhouse bathroom took away the feeling that she'd been tainted by her brief contact with the hideous object. She returned to find the doll gone. "I'm ready to hear about voodoo." She smiled at each of the men. "It's not like I haven't seen unpleasant sights."

"You've never dealt with pure, unmitigated evil, have you?" Not the gleam of a smile touched Terence's face.

"No, but since it's threatening my hospital and people I care about, I have to learn. Never let it be said a Best walked away from a good fight." She blushed at the blaze of admiration in Terence's eyes, but he sobered when he began.

"Like you, I knew little about voodoo until I went to Haiti. If I thought about it at all, I suppose I felt smug, even disinterested. After all, Haiti's thousands of miles away. I had enough in my life to keep busy without conjuring up a bunch of mumbo-jumbo stuff.

"Within a week from the time the ship docked, I was one smarter and sadder guy. Voodoo in Haiti is a fact of life."

He paused and Lindsey asked, "What is it, exactly? I'm like you were as far as having any real knowledge."

"It's insidious, terrifying, and practiced by a vast number of persons!" Terry slammed a fist into the open palm of his other hand. "From what I could determine, only a small percentage of the Haitians follow other religions—most among that minority are Roman Catholics."

Lindsey felt her heart race.

Terry continued. "Voodoo is a strange combination of Christian and African beliefs and superstitions. Initiation ceremonies include drumming, dancing, and animal sacrifices." His mouth turned grim. "Part of the appeal is that voodoo teaches believers can be possessed by gods during their rites. I'll never forget witnessing one such ceremony. A former voodoo follower who converted to Christianity sneaked a buddy and me close enough to get a good look." Terry took in a ragged breath.

Lindsey found herself clenching her hands in sympathy at the sorrow and disgust etched into his face. "Wh-what would have happened if you'd been caught?" she faltered.

"I don't even want to think about it. It's one of the most foolish, dangerous thing I've ever done but I needed to see for myself. Well, I did." He paused, obviously remembering. "Night in Haiti can be as black as voodoo itself. I'll skip the animal sacrifice part." His face showed revulsion and Lindsey bit her lip.

"The houngan—voodoo priest—drew designs on the ground, using flour. People began to dance. They believe they must do so until a god temporarily possesses at least some of them. They have a pagan god for everything: love, war, farming, rain, and so on. Before long, the frenzy grew until I wondered that God Himself didn't strike those involved down. I personally couldn't differentiate between those who supposedly became possessed and the rest of the howling horde, yet the horrible fascination of it all kept me from moving.

"At last my friend tugged at my arm and whispered, 'We must go. Now. They must not find us here and soon the ceremonies will fade and die.' We slipped away but I will never forget it."

"How can anyone practice such evil?" Lindsey cried out.

"Many of those who follow cannot read. They follow the teachings that have been handed down for generations. They're crammed into the country's overcrowded mountain valleys and coastal plains, living in one-room huts of sticks covered with dried mud, with thatched roofs. They exist on what yams, beans, corn, and rice they can raise. A few have pigs, or chickens, perhaps a goat."

Lindsey's heart ached for the faraway people. God had created them in His own image and loved them as much as He did her.

"There are always those who try to escape. That's why boatload after boatload sets out hoping to reach America and freedom from poverty, oppression, death. Many sink." The saddest look Lindsey had ever seen on a human face crept over Terence's countenance.

"Human life is less valuable than a farm animal. My converted Haitian friend told how an ill-clad man and woman jammed themselves into an already filled boat. She carried a squalling baby; he had a squealing pig over one shoulder. The man in charge curtly ordered them to get rid of excess baggage." He stopped to clear his hoarse throat.

Lindsey felt her fingernails dig into the palms of her hands. Her nerves screamed in protest against what she sensed would come.

"Well?" Shane O'Shea's voice cracked like a rifle shot.

"The man held the pig in a death grip, snatched the child, and threw it into the heaving waves."

"Oh, how could he do it?" Tears dripped, but Lindsey made no effort to wipe them away.

"That's what I asked my friend. He looked sad. 'The man knows he can have other children. He also knows he will probably never again have a pig.'"

The fire in the fireplace sullenly hissed. Lindsey shivered.

"It is a bleak picture," Shane said from the shadows.

"There is some hope," Terry quickly said. He stood, threw another log on the fire, and settled back on the rug next to Lindsey. "Christianity is nibbling away, often through schools and sponsorships, anything to improve the cycle of poverty and hopelessness. Medical personnel who dispense healing also cast doubt on the validity of witch doctors. These things are having an impact. There are those, more than you would believe, who learn about Jesus and turn to Him. Yet each step is hard won."

He flung his arms wide. "How do you combat centuries-old fear? Voodooists believe gods, demons, and spirits of the dead rule the world. Foremost among them is Baron Samedi, ruler of the graveyard spirits. I personally talked with those who swore they had seen him, complete with the black suit and bowler hat he is said to wear.

"Then there is the need to always be on the alert, to ward off magical hazards. Voodooists hate and fear noon, for people cast no shadow. Their belief is, when a person's shadow vanishes, one's soul has also left the body and opened the door to inhabitation by unwanted spirits. Casting spells and wearing charms are said to ward off enemy attack, such as dolls made in the victim's likeness. Other spells and charms are used to ensure good crops, cure illness, make a desired one love the wearer. The list is endless. Can you see how impossible it is for those drenched in-those beliefs since childhood to break free? There is also the fear of reprisal to self or family if one disavows voodoo."

For the second time that evening, Lindsey felt contaminated. No wonder Terry had asked if she really wanted to know all this horrible stuff. "Now it has touched Shepherd of Love. Why? Is the hatred of those in Haiti who resented you so strong it can travel this far?" Excitement stirred within her. "Terry, first thing tomorrow there's something you should do."

"What?" He raised one eyebrow and the corners of his mouth turned down. "Call an assembly and announce someone has a vendetta against the new chaplain?" His sudden grin took any possible string from his suggestion.

"No." She felt red spots leap to her face. "Call some of the people from the hospital mission ship and casually work the conversation around to voodoo. They will surely mention it if they have received similar—uh—gifts."

"Hey, great idea!" He beamed at her. "That way we may narrow it down. If they haven't, it means—"

"—one of two things," his father interrupted. Firelight gleamed in his blue eyes as Shane ticked the possibilities off on his fingers. "One: you're being targeted because of the spiritual work you did rather than simply being part of the medical team. Two: it's a warning to the hospital instead of you."

"I'd hate to think that." Terry looked shocked.

"We can't rule it out." Shane glanced from Terry to Lindsey and grinned. "How am I doing as a silent partner in your co-detecting?"

"I'm not sure there's such a word, but you're doing fine," she told him.

Terry stood and extended a hand to help her up. "I'd better get you back to the hospital or you won't be fit for duty tomorrow." His eyes shadowed. "I know one thing. We have to find and stamp out this spark of evil before it kindles and becomes a conflagration." He fetched Lindsey's denim jacket and held it so she could slip into its cozy warmth.

"Come again, lass. Any time."

As Lindsey followed Terence out to his car, Shane's invitation curled down into her heart like a tired child in her mother's lap. She wistfully glanced back at the old white farmhouse, wondering what it would be like to live there, secure and protected from the human misery she saw every day. Yet she knew if that same house could talk, what tales it would share of birth and death, family squalls and sunny stretches, hope and despair, sickness and health.

Terence and Lindsey didn't talk much for the first few miles on the way home but maintained a comfortable silence. She had a feeling part of him had returned to Haiti, a suspicion confirmed when he said, "I honestly hope this whole thing is aimed toward me. I'd hate to have Shepherd of Love hurt." He paused then added in a low voice, "If I decide there is any chance of my bringing trouble to the hospital, I'll resign immediately."

"Don't be an idiot!" Lindsey blurted out. "The voodoo doll was obviously left to drive you away." The thought crept into her active mind. "Suppose you walk, thinking it's the best thing for the hospital. That may be exactly what someone wants you to do." The idea grew like Jack's beanstalk. "Terry." She laid her hand on his right arm, careful not to disturb his control of the wheel. "How do we know who they might plant here in your place?"

"They? Plant? You make it sound like a conspiracy," he scoffed. "I can't believe such a thing could happen."

"Your father does, and he's one sharp person," she softly reminded.

"Yeah." Terence sighed. A thoughtful note replaced his Doubting Thomas attitude. "Like Dad said, Satan's biggest targets are those who serve God best. Shepherd of Love certainly qualifies in that department."

Lindsey's mind raced ahead of him. She took her hand

from his sleeve and turned toward him within the confines of her seat belt. "Play devil's advocate for a few minutes, will you? Suppose, God forbid, you are Satan. You're pledged to doing everything you can to win souls to your cause. You will roll over anyone and everything in your way, a juggernaut relentlessly championing the cause of wickedness, heartbreak, and evil. You have eyed a certain Seattle hospital for a long time. The very name is abhorrent to you. Shepherd of Love, called for the Son of God. How you hate Him! Even though you've won some major battles, He's bested you through the ages. Bah, what good is winning battles when you know you are losing the war?"

She gave her imagination free reign. "Month after month, year after year, the hospital negates your most diabolical schemes. You are determined to smash its usefulness forever. How? By using the cunning that first brought sin into the world and has grown ever since. What will you do to rid yourself of Shepherd of Love, the albatross around your neck that causes you to grind your teeth each time you behold it?"

Terence waited so long to answer she wondered if he thought her mad to suggest such an exercise, even in the interest of solving the mystery. At last he spoke.

"I'd attempt to infiltrate one of my henchmen into the hospital itself and order him to do his best, no, worst." He glanced at her and back to the freeway. "How many new personnel have been hired in the past few months besides Dr. Keppler and me?"

Lindsey shook her head. "I have no idea, but we don't have a real high turnover." She tried to recall unfamiliar faces in the dining room but her frequent change of shifts meant it took time before she noticed the newer employees.

"There's no real way of finding out without rousing suspicion," Terence grumbled.

"What else would you do?"

"Attack at the hospital's weakest point," he promptly told her.

"Which is?"

"The feeling of security and well-being that all is well simply because it's Shepherd of Love."

Lindsey sat up as though a pitcher of ice water had been dumped down her back. "You don't mean it!"

"Of course I do. Don't get me wrong. I don't think we have a bunch of naive doctors, nurses, and other workers at the hospital. But I do feel because of the requirement that only dedicated Christians be hired, over a period of time an attitude has developed that could leave the hospital vulnerable. Remember how you felt when you first saw the voodoo doll? Partly because of what it was, of course, but remember your exact words? 'What—it's not—it can't be . . . At Shepherd of Love? Impossible!'"

His exact imitation sent more chills down his companion's spine. After a moment she found her voice and weakly explained, "It's just that I was stunned and unprepared."

"My point exactly. Lindsey, every decent person, Christian or not, like it or not, is in a war." His voice softened and he touched her hand lightly before returning his own to the wheel. "It's easy to forget that, when things are going along fine. Good people quote, 'Why look for evil? It will come soon enough.' There's merit to the thought; it's even supported by scripture. On the other hand, terrible things happen when we let down our guard against them."

She had no reply. Neither could words have escaped her constricted throat. The truth of what he said burned into her, along with a great fear. Were the hospital and friends she loved playing ostrich, burying their heads in the sands of good works while unknown forces threatened?

At her outside apartment door, she raised a troubled gaze to the young chaplain. "Thank you," she whispered. "I can't honestly say I enjoyed all of the evening; some has been too disturbing. I did love meeting your father and having dinner with both of you."

Terence looked down the short distance to her upturned face. "What big eyes you have, Grandmother." A twinkle came to his own. "Someday after we solve our mystery I . . ." He bent his head. Just before his lips met hers, the sound of laughing voices came from the parking lot behind them. He stepped back, an exasperated look on his face.

"Lindsey, Terry. Where have you been? Have you heard the news?" Patti ran to them on frivolous, high-heeled blue shoes that matched the wool dress peeping from beneath an unbuttoned raincoat. "Isn't it awful?" An air of excitement radiated from the blonde nurse, but Lindsey suspected it came as much from Bart Keppler's presence at Patti's side as from whatever world-shaking news she carried.

"News?" Terry's strong fingers surreptitiously squeezed Lindsey's. She caught a note of warning in the quick glance he shot toward her.

"Yes. Someone sent a death threat to Nicholas Fairchild." Patti's round blue eyes displayed shock and genuine affection. "It's on every TV station in Seattle and even the major networks have picked it up. How did you miss it?"

"I took Lindsey home with me for dinner and we didn't have the TV on," Terry explained. His fingers tightened on Lindsey's. "What did the note say?"

"The police aren't releasing the contents." Dr. Keppler looked furious. "Of all the stupid things to do, this is the worst. Fairchild's one of the most loved men in Seattle. Doesn't the jerk who did it know the entire city will be up in arms?"

Score one for Black Bart, Lindsey thought. Either he belongs on stage receiving an Academy Award for Best All-time Actor, or he is genuinely distressed. I'd hate to be in the note-sender's shoes and have all that anger turned on me.

Patti fell silent, a jolted expression on her pretty face.

Lindsey suspected she'd never seen the handsome doctor in such a rage. Patti's eyes looked the size of the dinner plates in a doll's tea set.

Doll. Voodoo doll. The whole appalling day flashed through Lindsey's mind, leaving her suddenly tired. If only she didn't have to work tomorrow. She might be twenty-four years old but right now she wished she were four or eight or fourteen, surrounded by the parental love that chased away monsters.

Things that go bump in the night don't even come close to the terror voodoo creates—and not just in its followers, Terry had said. Now she understood. A caricature doll with a pin through its heart. A death threat against one of the finest Christian men she'd ever known. Foreign, terrifying happenings in the formerly peaceful hospital that existed only to serve. She slumped against the door.

"Lindsey, are you all right?" Patti tore herself free of the arm Dr. Keppler had draped over her shoulders and shook her friend. "You look like the original Ice Maiden."

She forced herself to laugh. "I'm okay. Just shocked and angry, like Dr.—Bart. If you don't mind, I'll hit the shower."

"Good night, Lindsey. Try to get some sleep," Terence told her.

She wanted to ask just how she was supposed to do that, but decided against it. With this new crisis in what Terry had laughingly dubbed the *Secret at Shepherd of Love,* could she ever again sleep within the walls of the staff residence hall and not feel surrounded by nameless, encroaching evil?

eleven

The next morning, Terry put in a series of random calls to those with whom he had served in Haiti. "An advantage to living on the West Coast," he remarked as he hung up the phone. "I can call when dawn's still in the eastern sky without rousing Eastern friends from their beds."

Shane grinned and flipped smoking hot griddle cakes onto his son's plate. Always an early riser, he persisted in getting breakfast—over Terry's protests. "People die in bed," he always retorted to Terry's protests. "You miss the best part of the day by sleeping in. Besides, I can take a nap later."

"You can but you probably won't." Terry would say.

And Shane's eyes would twinkle as he answered, "If I get tired enough, I will."

Once the routine had been established, Terry found it charged his batteries for the day. He knew his father also treasured their leisurely breakfast, quiet talk, brief scripture reading, and prayer.

This particular morning Terry had made six calls before breakfast. All his former associates sounded delighted to hear from him, urged him to come visit when he could, and anxiously inquired about his father. Terry didn't mention the voodoo doll incident. He did casually ask during each conversation, "Any more trouble with the witch doctors after I left?" He figured that questions would open the door in case someone else had been harassed since the mission ended and the participants returned home.

Every answer was the same: threats by disgruntled witch doctors, minor vandalism such as voodoo signs drawn on the ground near where the medics worked, but no actual attacks.

"Not even voodoo dolls?" Terence kept his voice light.

110

"No. Nothing to concern or stop us," came the reply each time.

Terry took a bite of griddle cake, little wiser than he had been before the calls. "So either it's the religion thing or the hospital that's being targeted, just as you suspected." He drew his brows into a straight line. "Last night Lindsey came up with a knockout." Between bites, he repeated the weird conversation they'd had on the way home, including her challenge that had led to their brainstorming session. He did not add that Dr. Keppler and Patti's arrival had cheated him of a kiss he knew would have been far more than a casual good-night salute. With each passing day, the attraction and admiration he felt for Lindsey grew.

He grinned. Why bother telling his father anyway? Dad read him as well as he read the scriptures. He probably knew more about a certain chaplain's heart murmurs at this point than his son did.

Keen blue eyes stared into Terry. "Be careful, son. Very careful. Warn her again not to mention the doll incident to even her most trusted friends."

"That's one of the problems." He quickly sketched in Patti's growing involvement with Dr. Keppler. His face took on a thoughtful expression. "Lindsey didn't say so, but I know he's been after her. Now it appears he's using Patti to get back at Lindsey for rejecting him."

"You don't like him, do you?"

"No." It came out flat and hung in the room. "I don't know why and it bothers me." He considered for a moment. "Maybe he's just too—"

"Just too what?" Shane patiently prodded.

"Too good-looking. Too seemingly all together. Too good to be true. Too in control." Terry laughed at his strange reasoning.

"Has he ever been in Haiti?"

Terry shrugged. "Who knows? And I don't see how I can find out."

His father gave him a shrewd gaze and a little grin. "Wait until he's at the same table in the dining room, then regale those there with stories of your mission. It's natural for you to want to share and I guarantee they will be interested. Some more than others." Shane leaned forward, a blood-hound look on his face. "Be sure to mention the persecution, any run-ins with voodooists, then watch the faces of those around you, but don't let anyone notice what you are doing."

He broke off to look at the clock. "Enough mystery. There's just enough time for devotions." They followed their Bible reading with fervent prayers enlisting God's help in extinguishing the spark of evil in the hospital and ended with a special prayer for Nicholas Fairchild's safety.

❧

Driving to work, Terence rehearsed several ways to introduce the subject of Haiti into table conversation. During the time he'd been at Shepherd of Love, he, Bart Keppler, Lindsey, and her two best friends had formed the habit of drifting to the same table whenever their shifts allowed. A variety of other employees occupied the other two seats, again depending on work schedules. His heart beat faster. He felt a smile curve his lips. Lindsey would be at both lunch and dinner since she was on day shift.

The next instant he frowned. Could he steal a minute with her ahead of time to warn her what he planned to do? If someone, anyone within hearing distance, had knowledge of yesterday's incident, the slightest stir on Lindsey's part might turn suspicion toward her. "God, am I wrong to let her become involved?" His hands tightened on the wheel and he changed lanes to let a merging car onto I-405. He shook his head. Now wasn't the time to be questioning. He hadn't been able to dissemble about finding the voodoo doll and once she saw it, Lindsey was involved—for better or worse.

His irrepressible sense of humor returned the laugh to his

lips. "For better or worse? Strangely familiar, Lord." Daydreams dismissed worry. God willing, one day Terence O'Shea would echo the same changeless vows he had asked so many couples to repeat. Would Lindsey Best be the woman who responded to the charge, with unbreakable vows of her own? Her piquant face danced in his mind, strangely untouched by all the heartbreak she had seen in her nursing career. He was overwhelmed with the desire to protect her from every ugly thing, but he knew he could not. He must do what he could and leave Lindsey's safety and happiness in the hands of One who loved her better than life itself.

To Terry's chagrin and disappointment, he failed to see Lindsey before lunch. A heavy surgery schedule kept her too busy for interruptions and just when he thought he might contact her, a grieving couple hesitantly came into the Chapel with a story that never lost its pathos. A hit and run driver, apprehended a few miles down the highway, unsteady from booze, wild with fear and remorse. The crumpled form of a child beside a road. Screaming rescue vehicles with paramedics who shook their heads, unable to do anything except carry the lifeless body away and notify the parents.

How many times had he heard it before? When would it end, the senseless destruction of innocent life by those who bragged they could hold their liquor?

"We believe in God, but we can't understand," the child's mother sobbed.

"He was our only child," the young father brokenly added. He gathered his wife in his arms and they clung together.

Terence simply listened for a long time before he quietly said, "No one ever understands such things." He placed a hand on each bowed head, praying for the right words, the way he'd prayed dozens of times before. He started to tell them as he had many others that God understood their

agony; He, too, lost an only Son. No, that should come later
Instead he prayed, "Father, I come to You seeking a blessing for these, Your children. Cover them with a blanket of
peace. Give them strength in this time of tragedy. Fill them
with assurance of Your love. Help them comfort one another. In Christ's name, amen."

A chaplain in the best sense of the word, Terence waited
encouraging them to cry, to find the natural release God
had created to help dull pain. When they quieted, he helped
them focus on making arrangements. Just having something
to do often brought temporary relief. He promised to see
them through this dark time, and he gave them his home
number. "If you can't reach me here, don't hesitate to call,"
he urged. "Dad will always know how to contact me."

An hour later they wordlessly wrung his hands and walked
away. He watched them go, arms around each other for support, shoulders bowed. Never again would life be the same
Terence sighed. Would their marriage last? Statistics, hard
and uncaring, showed many marriages did not survive the
death of a child. His fine lips tightened. This couple would
not be split apart by their grief, if he could help it. He'd see
they got the grief counseling anyone losing a loved one
desperately needs.

His appetite gone, Terry avoided the dining room. Time
enough later to institute his plan. Right now he must be re-
filled to meet whatever challenges this afternoon held. He
went into the small office adjoining the Chapel and closed
the door except for a crack wide enough to alert him if someone entered the larger room. He knelt, letting God read his
heart rather than trying to put thoughts and feelings into
words. The accident had victims other than the stricken
child, he realized now. The driver. His family. The young
man must live with what he had done. Crippled by guilt
would he ever be able to accept God's forgiveness? Or his
own? Terence lifted him up to God.

The afternoon hours remained mercifully free. After his

time of renewal, Terry tackled his mountain of reports and sighed with satisfaction when he finished the last one. "Good! I can see my desktop again." He stretched, feeling hollow, and his stomach growled. No wonder. Almost twelve hours had passed since he had been stuffed on Dad's griddle cakes. He headed toward the dining room, unsure whether he wanted to broach the subject shoved out of his mind by more recent events.

He didn't have to decide. Conversation around the table was taken up with the death threat to the hospital founder. In addition, both Dr. Keppler and Patti were conspicuously absent. A nod from Lindsey in response to his lifted eyebrow confirmed his suspicions that they were together. Again. An uneasy feeling drifted into Terence's heart like wraiths of fog over Puget Sound. Even if Keppler were not what he seemed, it didn't necessarily mean he meant to harm Patti. So why did Terry feel cold inside, thinking of the pert blonde nurse Lindsey considered an extra sister? He glanced at her and noted her expression betrayed the same concern he felt. He must see her alone—and soon.

Supper ended and Shina grinned impishly. "I think I'll run along. See you later, Lindsey." The others at the table also disappeared, leaving Terry exultant. He glanced around the nearly deserted dining room. No one was close enough to eavesdrop if they kept their voices low.

"I'm glad for the chance to talk with you," he began. "About last night—" He stopped abruptly when a tide of red color swept into her face. "No—I didn't mean—It's not what you think." She blushed again and Terry felt his pulse quicken. If he read the signs right, Lindsey Best was not indifferent to him.

"So what is my co-detective up to?" she wanted to know.

"I told Dad what we discussed. He suggested I casually bring Haiti into the table conversation one of these times. You know, spill over with enthusiasm about how much good the medical mission teams do, that kind of thing, then watch for reactions. He also said to warn you to be very careful. We may not even see more than the tip of the iceberg moving toward the hospital—and us."

"I've been thinking of that all day in between surgeries," Lindsey admitted. Her hazel eyes reminded Terry of the quiet pool beneath a maple where he had once lazed away summer days, dreaming of what he'd do when he grew up. He sighed. Never had his boyish imagination conjured up a brush with voodoo. A creeping chill caused him to say, "Lindsey, do you have vacation time coming?"

She blinked at the blunt change of subject. "At least a week."

"It might be well if you took it."

Understanding sprang to her face and a hint of contempt. "What do you think I am, a coward who turns and runs?" she demanded.

"Sorry," he mumbled. "I feel responsible for getting you into this mess. For a minute I thought—"

Her resentment died as quickly as it had been born and her eyes softened. "Thanks, Terry, but I'll stand and fight."

"I knew you would."

She cocked her head to one side and wrinkled her freckled nose at him. "Think I'm going to miss out on the chance of a lifetime to be an amateur detective? No way. I'll out-Nancy Nancy Drew and out-Hardy the Hardy Boys, if that's what it takes to solve our mystery!"

He found himself laughing in spite of his worry.

In the November darkness, he walked her through the covered passage from the hospital to the staff residence building. They slowly went down the long hall toward her apartment, absorbed in their low, continuing conversation. Terry fully intended to get the delayed goodnight kiss when they reached her door.

Again his plans were rudely torn asunder, in a way neither could have predicted.

"What on earth?" Lindsey stared at the garment bags, suitcases, and other personal possessions littering the hallway. Her face whitened. Shina, arms crossed in a belligerent attitude, stood glaring at Patti, whose face reflected a mixture of guilt and unease.

Lindsey raced toward them. Terry's footsteps pounded close behind. "What's happening?" she panted.

Patti's rounded chin elevated but she didn't meet her roommate's gaze. "Shina's upset because I'm moving into the cream and blue apartment." She added defensively, "It will give us both more privacy."

Lindsey felt she'd been hit in the stomach. Memory of a conversation weeks before replayed in her mind.

Herself: "You'd leave me?"

Patti's mysterious retort: "One never can tell," followed by a warm, "Of course not. . .even though you boss me."

The same nameless fear that flickered then burst into firestorm. "What brought this on? Why didn't you tell me?"

Bart Keppler loomed tall, dark, and triumphant in the doorway, arms filled with more of Patti's belongings. The malice in his dark eyes little resembled his honey tones. "Patti knew her changing suites would cause an argument. She also knew she couldn't hold out against your stronger personality," he smoothly explained. "Don't look so stricken, Lindsey. Having her live a few doors away doesn't change anything, does it?"

It changes everything, Lindsey wanted to shout. *Stronger personality? What about the influence you're having on her right this minute?*

Patti looked anxious. "It's for the best. This way I won't disturb you when you're trying to sleep after night duty."

"You never did."

Her friend shot a pleading glance at Bart. He promptly came to her rescue. "It's nice of you to say so, but things will be better this way. Patti isn't a little girl who needs a nanny. She's a grown woman who wants to be more independent, that's all. Why act as if the world just ended?"

"It really won't make any difference, Lindsey." Patti rushed to her on flying feet and hugged her, but the other nurse knew all this came from Black Bart's desire to get even. That knowledge left her standing stick-straight, arms at her sides, until Patti loosed her hold and stepped back. Her lips trembled like those of a rejected child.

"You are crazy," Shina accused. Her midnight-black eyes flashed and she looked more than ever like a beautiful Japanese doll, miraculously brought to pulsing, protesting life.

Patti didn't say a word. She simply turned, picked up some of the clutter, and marched to the end of the hall. Load after load she and Bart moved. Patti remained silent. Bart kept up an endless patter of repeated explanations. At last Patti disappeared into the cream and blue suite, and Bart came back, gathered the last armful, and hurled the final insult.

"If you can't swing the cost of the apartment alone, Patti is prepared to pay the difference, at least until you can find a roommate," he condescendingly said. "She doesn't want to put you in a financial bind."

Could people explode from sheer fury? Lindsey tried to speak and failed.

Not so Terry. His voice slashed like a sword. "Whose idea is that?" The arm he had lightly laid over her shoulders tightened. Lindsey would wager right now he longed to mop up the spotless hall with a certain hospital director.

"You're out of line, O'Shea." For a single moment, Keppler's facade slipped. The next, he laughed. "This is ridiculous. Patti wants and needs a change. Period. Why make a tragedy out of it?"

It is a tragedy, Lindsey wanted to say. Only Terry's warning squeeze of her shoulders kept her from raging. She managed a laugh. "Right. Why make a tragedy, when there are enough tragedies in the world—and hospital—already?"

"What's that supposed to mean?" Bart looked amused. "Oh, you mean the death threat to the director, I suppose." He shrugged. "There are always crazies out there. They'll do anything to get TV and newspaper coverage. Well, good night." He vanished inside the door of Patti's new apartment and firmly closed the door.

"I'll be happy to move in with you, if you like," Shina offered. The glisten of tears just beneath the surface made her lovely eyes darker than ever.

"Thanks." Lindsey took a deep breath. "That would be great, but let's just leave things for a time." She found it impossible to believe this was happening. Or that Patti wouldn't come to her senses and back where she belonged.

A look of understanding filled Shina's face. She held out her arms. Lindsey flew into them, towering over the tiny nurse but glad for the comfort.

Terence said good night and left. Shina trailed Lindsey into her apartment and silently stood by while the taller nurse opened the door to a room empty of everything except the furniture furnished by the hospital. The bed looked naked without the puffy comforter Lindsey had curled up on too many times to count. She turned on her heel, walked out, and closed the door behind her. Reality set in. Patti had actually gone, blinded by infatuation, manipulated by a master.

"He really is Black Bart, isn't he?" Shina observed from her perch on the end of the couch. Trouble underlined every word.

"He appears to be." Lindsey curled more firmly into the opposite end. The desire to tell Shina everything nearly overpowered her. She stifled the words, but vowed to ask Terry at the first possible minute if they could make Shina part of the detective team. Small she might be, but Shina possessed one of the keenest minds in the hospital. She could be a real asset.

twelve

"When Patti moved to the end of the hall, she might as well have taken up residence on Mars," Lindsey bitterly complained to Shina one evening, just before going on duty. Still on swing, she only caught brief glimpses of her former roommate. The fleeting encounters were not reassuring. A certain reserve had fallen over the blonde nurse and a wary expression had replaced the candid, trusting gaze that made Patti so attractive and loved.

"I see her more than you do, but we never really talk." Shina took a couple of extra steps to keep up with Lindsey's longer stride. "I'm trying not to rock the boat." She giggled. "I never thought I'd say this, but I miss her chatter. So do others. They even give her a bad time about it. She just smiles, as if she knows a wonderful secret but won't tell."

Lindsey stopped short. "You don't think she's engaged, do you?"

"I hope not. I get the feeling Dr. Keppler's using her, although I can't figure out how or why." She twisted her fingers. "There's something else. He cornered me the other day and said in that butter cream voice of his, 'I haven't seen you going out with anyone lately, Shina. I assume this means you're no longer engaged. How does dinner sound?'"

Lindsey gulped. "What did you say?"

Shina's eyes twinkled. "I was saved by the bell—actually, the intercom paging him. I've been avoiding him ever since."

"Maybe you shouldn't."

Her mouth opened wide. "Are you out of your mind?"

"No." Lindsey couldn't explain that the invitation might

be the bolt of lightning needed to get her and Terry's investigation going again. There had been no opportunity so far to tell him she believed Shina should be taken into the sleuthing team. Terry had extended his duties into after-hours, spending time with the hit-and-run driver and the couple who had lost their child.

His one attempt at mentioning Haiti netted a big, fat zero. There had been interest and questions, but no particular reaction. Dr. Keppler frankly admitted, "You're more altruistic than I, O'Shea. I can't imagine even going to that hotbed of radicals and mumbo-jumbo, let alone infuriating the local witch doctors."

One of the interns at the table commented, "You don't have to go clear to Haiti to find mumbo-jumbo. New Orleans is lousy with it and if what I hear is true, it's creeping in a lot of other places."

"Such as?"

Keppler's patronizing question brought a flash of resentment to the intern's eyes. "Such as right here. There are some strange things going on in the hospital." He clamped his lips shut, and Lindsey got the feeling he wished he hadn't allowed Bart to goad him into speaking.

"Such as?" Keppler repeated, his eyes slitted in amusement.

"I'm not saying anything yet but I'm sure keeping my eyes and ears open," the other retorted. He glanced around the circle of watching faces. "The rest of you should do the same."

Dr. Keppler's face grew mottled. Angry sparks shot from his dark eyes. "If there's any mumbo-jumbo going on in my hospital, it's from delirious patients." He shoved back his chair. The sound grated into the sudden pool of silence like fingernails on a chalkboard.

Lindsey didn't dare look at Terry. Instead, she sneaked a glance at Patti. A horrified expression rested on her friend's face, much like the one she'd seen the other time Bart showed his rage.

She's slipping away from her friends, perhaps even from God, Lindsey thought.

Her worst suspicions were confirmed the very next day.

For the first time in days, when the three nurses gathered around the breakfast table, no one joined them. "Where's your troupe of admiring interns, Patti?" Shina teased.

The blonde nurse's face flamed. She raised her chin. "As if I care anything about those childish interns."

"Maybe you should." Lindsey wished she'd bitten her tongue.

Patti turned on her. Blue lightning blazed in her eyes, but she kept her voice low. "Just because you're jealous that Bart dumped you doesn't give you the right to put me down," she said furiously.

"Excuse me?" Lindsey couldn't believe her ears. Neither could she believe what her eyes saw. Patti had been hypnotized into believing every word he said.

"Don't deny it. Just because Bart believes differently than you do, you persecute him." Defiant red flags waved in her cheeks. "Let me tell you something. I agree with him. As long as a person is sincere, God will honor his or her beliefs."

"Wrong." Shina jumped into the discussion with both feet. "Adolf Hitler was one of the most sincere men who ever lived. So are all those who fight in the so-called 'holy wars.' You're trying to tell me God honors them?"

Patti sniffed but her expression showed doubt. "You would bring up exceptions. I'm talking about good people."

"Who are they?" Shina snapped, her manner so unlike her usual quiet, accommodating self that the others stared. "Remember, Jesus said that there are none good but one— God. What's happening to you, Patti?"

For the beat of a pulse, Lindsey thought their friend would crumble. She looked totally miserable, so much so Lindsey unwisely whispered, "Give it up, Patti. He isn't worth it."

Every trace of weakness fled. Patti's face turned rock-hard. "Bart Keppler is a fine, far-seeing doctor and man. I intend to marry him, if he asks me." She turned on Shina. "As far as your Bible quoting, everyone knows you can prove any point you want by picking and choosing scripture. Jesus was speaking in parables, as He often did." She pushed back from the table and walked out, but not before a lone tear escaped.

"She may argue all she wants about people having the right to believe the way they choose, but she doesn't believe it," Shina observed. She slumped in her chair, face strangely colorless even above her apricot pants uniform. "Desert Storm was a Sunday school picnic compared to the battle raging inside Patti."

"Early teachings warring with her feelings for Bart," Lindsey muttered. "I should have kept still."

"Yes, you should have," Shina frankly told her. "Right now, her mind's telling her you're a threat to her happiness. Her long friendship is shouting it isn't true. Don't you see? If she could simply write you off as jealous, all the nagging doubts about Black Bart would die. She can't. I pray she never will."

Lindsey stood. "I owe her an apology. Wonder if I can catch her before she gets to Outpatient?"

"Be careful how you approach her," Shina warned. Her smooth brow wrinkled with concern. "She's in love with the wonderful image she's created. Until she sees Dr. Keppler as he is, nothing will change that. One thing's in our favor. So long as he's asking other nurses out, he certainly won't marry Patti."

"See you later." Lindsey hurried out in search of Patti.

She didn't find her. When she got to Outpatient, she ran into Patti's supervisor. "What's chewing on Patti Thompson?" the exasperated charge nurse demanded. "She bursts in here, says she isn't feeling well and can't work. This isn't the first time. In the last few weeks, she's gone from my most dependable nurse to the least. As much as I'd hate to do it, if she doesn't pull herself together, I'll have to write her up." She shook her head, obviously concerned. "I hope it won't come to that. To my knowledge, she's never had a black mark on her record."

Lindsey's heart plummeted.

"Talk to her, will you?" The nurse swung away before Lindsey could say she was the last person in the world to talk with Patti Thompson right now.

Determined to see Terence, Lindsey headed for the Chapel. To her relief, the door of his study-office stood open. "Terry?"

"Here." He came toward her in long strides, obviously delighted to see her. "I miss you, Lindsey." He grinned and ruffled his mahogany-tinted hair. "I sound like my favorite nurse had been visiting Kalamazoo or points east, don't I? But you might as well have been for all I've seen you lately."

His open admiration soothed her troubled heart like mud on a bee sting. "Do you have time to talk?"

Terry's eyes turned poignant blue. "Of course. How about a drive?"

Wondering, Lindsey started to ask why they couldn't talk there in the Chapel. A quick shake of Terry's head, a forefinger held in the air, warned her. She swallowed her questions and said, "I report for work at—"

A second warning signal set her heart to thumping. So did Terry's hearty, "Good." He quickly put in a call to let the switchboard know he'd be away from the hospital for a time, caught up a jacket and his pager, and ushered her into the hall. To her amazement, he headed for the covered passageway leading to the staff residence building. "Get a warm coat," he told her. "You're being kidnapped."

Lindsey silently obeyed. Coat in hand, she glanced down the hall toward Patti's closed apartment door, tempted to knock.

Terence shook his head violently.

Sighing, Lindsey followed him out to the parking lot. A scowling sky filled with lowering clouds directly above Shepherd of Love promised a deluge. She shivered, remembering the ominous black clouds months before that had made her wonder if trouble for her beloved hospital lay ahead.

"Why the cloak-and-dagger act?" she demanded, once they were snugly belted into the station wagon and he started the motor. She longed for a reassuring grin.

It didn't come. Instead, Terry said, "What shift are you working?"

"Swing. Why?"

"Think your parents would give us space to hash out what's happening? The kids will be in school, won't they? Maybe your mother would even feed two starving hospital refugees lunch." He added irrelevantly, "Dad and I really want to meet your family. There just hasn't been time to invite them out to the farm."

"Of course, but I don't understand. Why now, today?"

He sent her a pitying look. "It's no longer safe to talk at the hospital, Lindsey. Not even in the Chapel or my office." He took his right hand from the wheel, fished in his jacket pocket, and laid something in her palm.

The closest she'd ever been to a bugging device was watching detective shows. Now she stared at the small eavesdropping tool with fascination. "Where did you get this? Why, there's dirt on it."

"Found it in a pot of flowers that appeared on my desk this morning."

"You just stumbled on it by chance?" She handed it back.

"No." His gentle voice contrasted strangely with the intrigue swirling through the hospital. "For the last few weeks I've been expecting some such thing." He grinned crookedly. "At least it isn't another voodoo doll."

She felt the weight of the world drop to her shoulders. "So it's real."

"Yes, and I have the feeling we haven't begun to see or comprehend the extent of what's going on." He dropped his hand over hers and squeezed, then returned it to the wheel. She knew the effort it took for him to lightly add, "Time for a ways-and-means meeting of the detective duo."

Her hand tingled from his quick grasp. "That's what I wanted to talk with you about," she eagerly said. In terse sentences she told him of Patti's outburst and that Dr. Keppler had invited Shina on a date. "Since she's already so much a part of this, I think we should tell her the whole thing and ask her to play Mata Hari."

"Would she consent to go out with him?"

"I think so, for such a worthy cause." An ice worm squiggled down Lindsey's spine and she sat up straight. "We're not putting her in danger, are we?"

He considered for a moment. "No reason to believe that, or I wouldn't agree. The things so far have been more harassment than dangerous."

She mulled it over.

"Do you think it would do any good for me to talk with Patti?" he asked.

"Maybe later." She stared out the windshield, where gray drizzle and the monotonous swish-swish of the wipers had a mesmerizing effect. "Right now, she'd feel Shina and I had set her up." Lindsey sighed, spirits at an all-time low. "I don't know what to do about the two-bedroom apartment, either. It's costing more than I can afford." Strange, how easy it was to discuss finances with the young chaplain and know he'd understand. "Shina promised she'd move in with me but she feels as I do. Once that happens, we've lost Patti. Although she left of her own accord, it's bound to make her feel the door has closed behind her and that there's no coming back, even if she wanted to."

"What do your folks say?" His rich, deep voice inspired confidences. No wonder he so successfully performed his chaplain duties.

"They're absolute angels. So are my brothers and sisters. I didn't tell them why Patti moved out, just that she did, but I hoped she'd be back. They immediately offered to help make up the difference." She blinked hard and a lump grew in her throat. "Every one of them said I was contributing entirely too much to the family coffers and the time had come for me to think more about myself. How can I, when they did so much to help me through nursing school?"

He countered with a question. "How much do you enjoy giving?"

She turned her gaze from the gloomy day and let it rest on his serious face. "What a strange question!"

"Not really," he disagreed. "They sacrificed for you because they loved doing it. In turn, you became a gracious giver. Don't turn into a grudging receiver, as so many do when faced with the need to accept rather than give. If you do, you rob your family—and others—of knowing the great joy of giving."

Lindsey felt hot color redden her cheeks. Grudging receiver. She'd never thought of it that way. On impulse she said, "You're right. Pride, I guess."

Terence smiled. "It usually is. I had to fight Dad every step of the way when I dropped out of the hospital ship mission and came home. If I remember right, I used the same terminology to him I just gave you in my mini-sermon." His grin widened into a hearty laugh. "All right, where do I turn?"

❧

Later that evening when Lindsey prepared for work, she faced her mirrored image and brushed her auburn hair. "If I live to be an old, white-haired lady I'll remember today. Not so much for what we did as the simple joy of being together. Dad and Mom adored Terry, and I. . ." Her fingers stilled. The eyes looking back at her opened wide. Tell-tale streaks of color surged into the freckled face. Recognition came on gossamer wings. "Lord, am I in love with Terence O'Shea?"

Yes, a little voice shouted inside her, so insistent it could not be denied.

When had it started, she wondered, this feeling that she wanted to spend the rest of her life with the young chaplain? To laugh and love, to weep and mourn; to bear his children and make a home; to work side by side with the man who had conquered her heart? Perhaps it began with the caring and tenderness he showed toward those he served. Or the evening at the farm, feeling at one with Terry and his father. Had her response lain dormant until this afternoon, when he kissed her in the warm privacy of the station wagon and circled her with strong, protecting arms she passionately wished would never let her go?

Love had not come with trumpet and drums, as her puppy-love fantasies once predicted. Instead, a tiny spark of friendship—fanned by trust and a shared love for the Master—had kindled in the fortress of her heart and sprung into a warm, enduring glow, to last a lifetime.

Lindsey had little time to examine her love throughout the following arduous hours. Patient after patient came up from Emergency, a result of the stormy night that had worsened after Terry and Lindsey got back from her parents' home. She remained far beyond the end of her shift, moving from task to task with strength so incredible she knew her Heavenly Father granted it to match the present need.

Two o'clock came and went. Three. At half-past, the surgeon in charge announced, "That's it. Thanks for staying, Lindsey. Now get out of here."

Stumbling with fatigue, the exhausted nurse didn't take time to shed her filthy scrubs but headed out the door. The corridor stretched silent and empty before her, eerie, frightening. "Don't be an idiot," she told herself. "You've walked this corridor a thousand times."

Not at this time of night, a horrid little voice reminded. *It's usually at the end of a shift, or when you're going for a break.* Nerves already strained near the breaking point by the excruciating previous hours, she morbidly whispered, "Perfect time and place for trouble." Great. That certainly didn't make her feel any better. She speeded her steps, unable to throw aside a suspicion of something sinister in the quiet building.

Lindsey's uneasiness increased when she neared a deserted nurses' station. It served as a hub for several ICU rooms spraying out like spokes in a wheel. A desk lamp cast a golden pool of light on a welter of papers cluttering the desk.

"Impossible!" Anger replaced Lindsey's debilitation. This particular station should not be unattended. From it, personnel monitored postoperative patients. Was she having a nightmare? She rubbed her eyes, but no genie appeared. Neither did hospital employees. She quickened her pace, reached the station, and quickly scanned the monitors, relieved to find nothing amiss.

Lindsey heard a low cry from one of the rooms. Heedless of her disheveled condition, she hurried inside. The night charge nurse, a kindly LPN, and a scared-looking student nurse stood by the bedside of a white-haired patient Lindsey recognized as Mrs. Landers, a recent gall bladder case.

"Get me out of here," the woman cried. Stark fear showed in her face.

"You're going to be all right, Mrs. Landers," the charge nurse told her.

"I'm not all right!" She struggled against the LPN's restraining hands. "How would you like to wake up and find a hooded figure hovering over your bed, mumbling incantations? Get me out of this hospital!"

"You must have had a nightmare," the LPN soothed.

"Why don't you believe me?" Mrs. Landers sobbed. "It really happened."

Lindsey's blood chilled. Post-op patients sometimes had bad dreams, but Mrs. Landers appeared more alert than one coming out of a nightmare. Then, too, why had the student nurse acted terrified? If only she could talk privately with her.

She had the chance when the girl emerged from the room and stumbled back to the desk at the nurses' station. "How is Mrs. Landers?" she asked.

"All right. They gave her something to help her sleep." The student dropped into a chair, glanced both ways, and confided in a whisper, "She wasn't dreaming. I saw it too, on the monitor. A dark figure bending over the bed. I told the charge nurse. She thought I was crazy, but she went to investigate."

It explained the abandoned nurses' station. It did not explain the mystery.

thirteen

Back and forth. Back and forth. If the telephone didn't ring in the next three minutes, the pacer wouldn't be there to hear it; he wasn't waiting in the cold any longer.

Hunched and furious, the dark figure rubbed freezing hands, trying to restore circulation. When the phone rang at last, he fumbled with the receiver with numb fingers.

No exchange of pleasantries this night. Not that there ever had been many. Now even the veneer of civility had vanished in mutual contempt. "What do you think you're doing? Are you trying to ruin everything we've worked for?" The harsh whisper echoed to the worn, barren rafters.

"You were getting nowhere," the other retorted.

"How is frightening an old woman half out of her wits going to help the Cause?"

"It's just the beginning." A click followed the jeering laugh, then buzzing, like a swarm of enraged bees. The listener held the phone so long a tinny voice droned, "If you'd like to make a call, please hang up and try again."

The receiver dropped with a little crash. As usual, the disembodied voice on the other end of the line had gotten in the last word. It always would.

❧

Heavy pounding on her door roused Lindsey from unfathomable depths of sleep into which she'd drifted after hours of tossing and turning. "Wake up!" The pounding increased in intensity. "Lindsey, open the door."

Lindsey lurched out of bed and through the living room. "Shina?" Her sleep-clouded eyes opened wide when she finally got the door unlocked. "Patti! What are you doing here?" She grabbed the door frame for support.

131

"There's terrible trouble." Patti's eyes were wide, her face pale. "Let us in, will you?"

Sleep fled before the terror in her friend's eyes. Lindsey helplessly sank to a chair. The other nurses, who looked as if they hadn't slept in a week, sat on the couch. "Tell her," Shina ordered.

Patti's eyes glazed over. "There's a conspiracy to destroy Shepherd of Love."

Lindsey felt as if she'd been kicked in the stomach. "Conspiracy?" Even in her wildest imaginings, she hadn't dreamed anything of this magnitude.

Patti licked dry lips. "Yes."

"How do you know?" Lindsey leaned forward, shaking. Shina tossed her an afghan from the couch. Lindsey gratefully wrapped it around her shoulders and sat on her feet to warm them.

"Remember what the intern said at the table about strange things happening? I didn't think anything more about it until after our argument at breakfast yesterday. I just couldn't work." Misery filled her face, but her blue gaze didn't waver. "I didn't want to run into either of you, so I took a different route from Outpatient and detoured past Emergency. Mike, one of the ambulance drivers who often brings patients in, stopped me in the hall."

She paused for breath and Lindsey's nerves screamed.

"Tell her what he said." Shina patted the blonde nurse's arm encouragingly.

"He wanted to know if I knew anything about an undercurrent here at the hospital." Patti licked her lips again. "In the past week, two different families refused to allow Mike to bring relatives to Shepherd of Love, even though it's the closest medical facility. He naturally asked why." Her voice dropped to a whisper. Her eyes looked enormous in her pinched face. "They told him they heard something strange was going on. Rumors about voodoo and patients being visited by hooded figures that make signs in the air and chant."

"What did you say?" Lindsey burst out.

Some of Patti's old spunk surfaced. "Told him it was absurd, of course. Mike promptly said voodoo dolls in the Chapel were more than absurd. He said everyone in the hospital knew Terry found a doll made in his image, tucked beneath the Bible on the Chapel altar. Is it true?" Her voice quivered.

No need for secrecy now. "Yes." How had word gotten around? Only she, Terence, and his father knew. Lindsey's world spun. What if her earlier suspicions hadn't been so far off, after all? The chaplain freely confessed he'd been in Haiti. Was his candor an excellent cover-up?

O ye of little faith, she flayed herself. She'd stake her life on Terence O'Shea being a man of God and incapable of duplicity. She must never let him know she had doubted him for one moment. His laughing blue eyes would change to fog-gray with hurt.

"Why didn't you tell us?" Shina asked Lindsey, but Lindsey only shook her head and remained silent.

Patti flushed and continued her story. "I was furious with you two and angry anyone would do such a thing. I needed time to think and was glad when I heard Lindsey leave with Terry. I skipped lunch, but by afternoon I couldn't stand myself. I decided to get away from the hospital. Bart—Dr. Keppler had given me a spare key to his sports car. He said I might want to drive it." She stared at her fingers. "I never had, but yesterday I needed to get away."

She looked up, face haunted. "I'd used up all my tissues crying, so I checked the glove compartment. No luck. Some people toss things under the seat. I groped underneath it. I didn't find tissues but something else." She shivered.

Why must Patti be so maddeningly slow? Lindsey longed

to shake her, even while her heart twisted with pity.

"Lindsey, he had a voodoo doll." She cast an imploring glance at Shina.

"The doll looked like you," the tiny nurse explained.

Lindsey couldn't speak.

"I put it in the exact spot I found it, made sure everything else was left undisturbed, came to my room, and tried to think. Later I heard Shina come in and told her. We knew you'd gone on duty and would be safe." Patti faltered. She stood and stumbled across to Lindsey. "Can you ever forgive me?"

"Of course." Lindsey hugged her friend. Their tears mingled.

"Even when I told myself you envied me because of Bart, I knew it wasn't true," Patti brokenly said. She wiped her eyes with the back of her hand. The childish gesture said more than words. "I also secretly felt glad Shina didn't move in with you, although I wouldn't admit it to myself. Lindsey, when I saw that doll with a pin through its heart I thought I'd die from pain." She sat up, took the tissue Shina sympathetically offered, and blew her nose.

"One good thing. It brought me to my senses. How could I swallow all that stuff Bart fed me? How could I believe he cared, or think I loved him?"

Shina softly repeated what she'd told Lindsey earlier. "You fell in love with what you thought he was."

Patti refused to be so easily excused. "I should have known better." She made a face before asking, "Now what?"

"Now I get a certain Terence O'Shea over here." Lindsey sprang for the phone, sent her SOS, asked for a half-hour to get cleaned up, and headed for the shower. Its fine spray washed away the last traces of exhaustion.

Shina busied herself in the kitchenette getting a late breakfast for Lindsey. Patti perched on Lindsey's bed while her friend dried her hair. "Please, mother, may I move back in now?" she meekly asked

"I don't think you should," Lindsey said from behind the auburn curtain of hair that hung over her forehead. She didn't notice the curious stillness from the end of the bed until she shut off the blow dryer and tossed her mane out of her eyes.

"I don't blame you for not being able to forgive me." Patti's bowed blonde head showed total defeat.

"It isn't that at all," Lindsey protested. "Stop and think. The minute you come back, the whole hospital will know."

"Including Bart Keppler." Patti's eyes showed understanding.

"Right." A fantastic idea crossed her mind. "Patti, would you and Shina mind giving me a few minutes with Terry before we talk?"

"Of course not." Patti tousled her hair and grinned in the old way. "I may be able to survive that long without being killed by curiosity."

Ten minutes later, Terry and Lindsey sat the other two nurses down and told them the entire story. Lindsey also reported the incident with Mrs. Landers and added, "It's interesting that outsiders knew about it before it happened."

"Maybe they didn't. I intend to have a talk with the intern who made the comments at the table. This may not be the first such happening." Terry looked grim. "Patti, did you ever want to be an actress? Ever take drama or participate in a school or church play?"

She looked at him warily. "A few times."

"How about you, Shina?"

"Ditto. Why?" She cocked her shining dark head to one side.

"If you're game, you might be of great help. I understand Dr. Keppler has asked you out?"

Shina slid an apologetic look at Patti. "Yes, but I didn't go."

Patti looked disgusted. "What a sheik! I must be the most gullible person who ever had the misfortune to cross his path. I hope I never see him again."

"Just be glad you found out now and not later," Terry told her. "Do you think you can keep from letting him know you suspect him?" He rumpled his hair.

"I don't think so." Patti sighed. "I'm not good at hiding my feelings."

"The other alternative would be for you to go on vacation. You mustn't take the chance of his finding out what you saw."

"You could ask for personal leave," Lindsey suggested. "Your supervisor would back you up. She's concerned about the quality of your work lately. I wasn't snooping," she quickly explained. "I went to Outpatient to apologize. . ."

"For my mistakes," Patti choked. "I know my work has slipped."

"I wanted to apologize to you for my mistake when I came on too strong at breakfast," Lindsey gently corrected. "But the charge nurse is genuinely concerned about you. So much she dreaded having to write you up and spoil your record."

"I made a mess of things, didn't I?"

"Who doesn't from time to tome? That's why forgiveness is so important," Terry counseled. Again Lindsey marveled at his ability to say the right thing at the right time. Would things ever settle down so they could spend time together, instead of being embroiled in unsavory doings?

"Do you think Black Bart is the hooded figure?" Shina inquired.

"I don't know," Terry confessed. "It will be interesting to see what he does about it. We won't have long to wait. The hospital's rocking with scuttlebutt about Mrs. Landers's nightmare visitor. Our acting hospital director has called a general staff meeting for this afternoon. We all have to go, especially you, Patti. Sit with Shina, if you like. Better yet, go with someone from Outpatient. It's crucial for you not to betray your change of heart toward either Lindsey or Dr. Keppler." He looked thoughtful. "You don't happen to have a sick or aged relative who could conveniently call you out of town, do you?"

"No." She took a long breath and expelled it slowly. "Am I in danger?"

"I honestly don't know." Terry looked somber and spread his hands in a gesture of helplessness. "We won't take any chances. So far, we aren't sure if Dr. Keppler is guilty of anything except producing voodoo dolls and that could be because—" He stopped abruptly.

"Don't try to spare my feelings," Patti cut in. She raised her chin, a mannerism as familiar to her friends as her blue eyes and blonde hair. "I know he can't stand rejection, especially by the female sex. At least part of what's been happening may be a getting-even thing because Lindsey turned him down." Her pretty lips tightened and her friends silently exchanged glances of relief. Evidently Patti's pride had been far more wounded than her tender heart.

a

That afternoon, hospital personnel assembled in the auditoriumlike meeting room like a gaggle of noisy geese. The summons for every person who could be spared from duty to attend, along with rumors of voodoo dolls and mysterious night visitors, generated speculation and even wilder rumors. Lindsey, seated next to Shina and a goodly distance away from an obedient Patti who came with Outpatient friends, felt sickened. Six months earlier, Shepherd of Love staff had good-naturedly discussed the latest engagement or how successful some new procedure had become. Now she saw dismay, even fear in the eyes of her coworkers.

Nicholas Fairchild stepped to the microphone. The last whispers died. Lindsey gasped. She'd expected to see the man bowed before the enormity of the calamity. Not so. Calm as a July morning, shoulders erect as a soldier, he faced the group that in all probability held at least one traitor. Lindsey had the feeling Nicholas had spent most of the day in prayer. Nothing else could account for his tranquillity.

"I am sorry to say hard times have come to us," he said simply. "Someone or ones appear bent on destroying the work we do here. We don't know who or why." He stepped away from the mike and his far-seeing blue eyes flashed. "I promise you this. We will find out!" His resonant voice filled the room.

A thrill of hope straightened slumped shoulders, lifted bowed heads, lightened heavy hearts. For a full minute, the hospital founder let his gaze roam from one side of the room to the other. It lingered on no one, yet Lindsey felt every person present must feel weighed. Who among them would be found wanting?

She stopped her mental woolgathering and disciplined a laugh when Nicholas said, "Bartholomew has a few words for us." How did the handsome acting hospital director like being addressed that way? She stared at the man striding forward, anticipating the moment when he turned to face those he supposedly served.

Shina's small, strong fingers dug into Lindsey's arm. "I can't believe it," she hissed.

Neither could Lindsey. Bart's face flamed with righteous indignation, eyes darker than obsidian in his white face. "Even the most Christian hospital cannot withstand evil forces if they are allowed to continue," he said, voice deadly. "Measures must be taken to discover and resolve any disturbing influence. I pledge to you to do my utmost to bring about the ultimate best for Shepherd of Love and all those who work and come here." He walked out, in a wild storm of applause.

Lindsey felt confused. Had the voodoo dolls only been a childish way of getting even? If not, how could Bart Keppler stand before them like an avenging angel bent on destroying evil? Lucifer himself couldn't have been more convincing. Lindsey had come to the meeting believing she'd see guilt in his eyes, a furtive flicker strong enough to confirm suspicion and expose Black Bart's masquerade. Instead, truth rang in his voice. Sincerity. He simply couldn't have been the hooded figure in Mrs. Landers's room.

Lindsey burned to get her codetectives' reactions, but she had no opportunity. Too many persons milled around her, praising Nicholas Fairchild and Dr. Keppler and expressing confidence that the whole thing would soon blow over. Even Shina could only lift one silky, questioning eyebrow. Lindsey had the feeling her small friend felt as muddled as she. A glimpse of Patti showed nothing but a bland mask. Good girl. The tight knot inside Lindsey loosened. At least Patti's eyes had been opened. No matter how innocent Bart was of frightening patients, Patti would neither forgive nor forget the hidden doll made in the likeness of her friend.

Terence O'Shea stood to one side, allowing the crowd to thin. Lindsey lingered as well. When everyone had gone, she started out, walking slowly enough for him to catch up.

"Are you headed for the dining hall?" he asked, voice loud enough to reach anyone who might be listening.

"Yes. I'm starved." Lindsey added in a whisper. "What do you think?"

"He's a clever man." Terry kept his voice low. "He also won the full support of almost everyone there. Did you notice the expression on faces around you?" She nodded and he continued. "Lindsey, everything he said is true. The catch is, it's all generalities." He ticked them off on strong, sensitive-looking fingers.

"One: Even the most Christian hospital *can't* withstand evil forces.

"Two: Measures certainly must be taken to discover and resolve this situation.

"Three: He pledged to do his utmost to bring about the ultimate best." Terry half-closed his eyes. "That gave me the creeps. Just what is Bart's utmost? What does he consider is the ultimate best?" He broke off at the dining room door.

They walked inside. Lindsey stopped short. Dr. Keppler sat between Patti and Shina at their usual table. She felt anger spurt. How dared he?

"Your feelings are showing," Terry warned. "Now is the time for all good detectives to put on their most guileless faces for the good of the mystery."

Laughing at his nonsense, she hastily adjusted her expression, chose food from the well-laden tables, and marched to the table. "Hello, everyone."

Bart and Shina responded. Patti studiously avoided eye contact and peppered her salad. Lindsey wanted to cheer. Transparent her friend might be, but Patti's loyalty would see her through a hard time.

"I've just been telling these charming ladies we need a break from this unpleasantness. I'd like to take you out for dinner as soon as we're all off at the same time." He cut into perfectly done roast beef. "Patti?"

She started to answer, raised her napkin, and sneezed. Lindsey suspected she'd deliberately taken the chunk of lettuce with the most pepper. Patti sneezed again.

"Doesn't sound like you'll be going out," Shina observed. "Better take a few days off and see if this develops into anything."

A third sneeze saved Patti the need to answer.

Lindsey hastily turned attention to herself. "I have tonight off, due to the extra hours I put in this morning, I am absolutely beat."

"Too bad." Bart laid his fork across his plate. "Were you by any chance in on the disturbance with Mrs. Landers?" He eyed her curiously.

"Uh huh." Lindsey forced herself to sound disinterested. "I finished in surgery super late—well, early." She yawned. "Still feeling it, by the way."

"So, what happened?"

"I didn't see anything except an upset patient and concerned nurses." *Good going, Lindsey,* she complimented herself. *You're turning into a master of evasion. Every word is the truth and nothing but the truth, if not the whole truth.* She bit back a grin.

Patti sneezed once more and excused herself. Lindsey had the feeling she felt herself on thin ice. Evidently Terence noticed it, as well. He immediately went into an amusing incident that had happened on the farm.

"Combite, huh?" Bart forked up the last of his chocolate cake.

"Excuse me?" The chaplain's eyes took on a terrier brightness.

"Interesting that you combine fun with your farm duties." He glanced at the wall clock. "I have to run." Never had his smile been more charming. "See you."

"Not if we can help it," Terry mumbled the minute Bart got out of hearing.

"Terry!" Shina's shocked whisper echoed Lindsey's reaction.

"Keppler's a first class liar," Terry whispered in a fierce voice. "He pretended ignorance of Haiti, but he just used the word *combite*. It's a Haitian word that describes how neighbors move from farm to farm, singing, planting, and harvesting." The chaplain's eyes gleamed with triumph. "That little slip is going to cost Black Bart dearly."

fourteen

A feeling of waiting stole through the hospital halls and into the rooms. To everyone's relief, no more hooded figures or voodoo dolls appeared. However, a rash of small incidents took place, each seemingly insignificant, all undermining the hospital's credibility.

"It's insidious," Terence told his father at breakfast. "No one knows how or why. Nothing's happening that can't be explained in a logical manner or attributed to human failure. Still, I can't help wondering what all this is leading up to and when it will end."

"For example?"

"Two different patients—one of them Mrs. Landers—complained to the charge nurse on duty that I didn't bother to come when they sent for me." His eyes took on a brooding look. "I knew nothing about their requests until the nurses called me personally. What could I tell the patients? That I may well be the victim of a conspiracy to help destroy Shepherd of Love's credibility?" He laughed harshly.

"Do you hold to the conspiracy theory?" The older man leaned forward in his chair, gnarled hands on the table.

"It can't be ruled out."

"Have you been able to figure out if it's you or the hospital that's under attack?"

"Probably both." Terry shook his head. "Dad, this is getting me down. There's also another problem. I don't know what Keppler will do if he finds out Patti Thompson saw the voodoo doll in his car. She took yesterday off, after sneezing at dinner." Some of his gloom lifted and his fine teeth flashed in a winning smile.

"Lindsey told me Patti shoved a forkful of well-peppered salad under her nose to keep from accepting Bart's dinner invitation. Shina innocently commented she should take time off. I wish she had an out-of-town friend or relative who needed her, so she could leave the hospital altogether."

"She does." Intrigue darkened the blue of Shane O'Shea's eyes.

"Who? She's racked her brains and not come up with anyone."

"Me," Shane promptly told his son.

"You?" Terry exploded with laughter.

"The same. Faith and begorra, lad, no one qualifies more. I'm out of town. Any friend of yours is a friend of mine."

"You don't need her."

"Oh?" Shane refused to abandon his idea. "Since when did a handsome Irishman like me not need a pretty colleen around to cosset him a bit?"

"It might not be such a bad idea at that," Terry agreed. "This is the last place Keppler would think of looking. Patti didn't let on she and Lindsey had made up their differences. Bart must know I'd be in sympathy with Lindsey." He shoved back his chair. "Dad, you're a genius." He laughed again. "Or maybe a knight in shining armor."

"Nay. Just a man who cannot abide the idea of an innocent maiden being harmed. Go fetch your friend." A canny look crept into his keen eyes. "If you really feel there's danger for her, don't tell anyone where she's to be." He paused. "Does the hospital require employees going on vacation to account for their whereabouts?"

"No."

"Good. The fewer people who know, the better. She'll naturally want to inform her parents so they don't send out an alarm, but have her call from here."

Terry seized on the idea. "She can tell them she's trying to avoid someone and if anyone calls asking for her address, not to give it. They can simply say she's out of town and they aren't sure when she'll be back. All true." He looked rueful. "It seems ridiculous for Lindsey and Shina not to know she's here."

"It isn't. One of them might be surprised into disclosing her whereabouts," Shane warned.

❧

Feeling like the lead character in a swashbuckler novel, Terence smuggled Patti and a well-packed suitcase out of her apartment under cover of darkness and the dinner hour. She acted glad to go. The past few days had taken their toll. She maintained a dispirited silence until they reached the farmhouse. However, the same atmosphere that had made Lindsey feel so at home weeks earlier gradually brought her peace.

She ate every crumb of the simple meal Shane offered, then insisted on doing the dishes and making up the bed in the guest room. Some of her sparkle returned. Terry had the feeling Patti was slipping out of a bad dream and back to normalcy.

"While I'm here, I intend to cook and clean to my heart's content," she earnestly told her hosts. "I'm a closet home-maker at heart." She fell silent and stared into the flames in the fireplace as Lindsey had done, curled up on the same braided rug.

True to her word, she did everything she could to fit into the family. Terry found himself looking forward to coming home at night to a house that bore an unmistakable woman's touch. After polishing off two pieces of pumpkin pie the third night she was there, he told her, "Miss Patricia Thompson, if I were not already smitten with your red-haired friend, I'd fall in love with you on the spot."

Her laugh sounded like the chime of bells in the wind. "Alas, kind sir, I fear 'twould only be for my pumpkin pie."

"Not true," he indignantly told her. "I also like your apple dumplings, baked salmon with dressing, and bread pudding."

She threw a dish towel at him and announced that for that he could load the dishwasher while she put things away.

When they finished, he laid one hand on her arm and looked into her eyes. "I meant what I said, Patti. Any man except one irrevocably in love with another woman would be proud to win your love."

The shine of tears softened her blue eyes. "Thanks, chaplain. I needed that right now. It's good to know." Her serious mood vanished. "Especially when you're robbing me of my best friend, if the wind's blowing the way I think."

He shamelessly decided to pump her for information. "You think I have a chance?" he anxiously asked.

"Maybe. Want me to put in a good word for you?" she teased.

"You repeat what I just said and you'll be in mega trouble," Terry warned with a mock frown. "When the time comes, I'll tell her myself."

Patti giggled and ran into the living room. "Help, your son is threatening me," she told Shane who sat watching with a half-smile.

"You don't look frightened."

"As if anyone ever could—here." A shadow crossed her expressive face, dampening her lashes. She raised her chin. "Let's forget all that while we can."

The next evening, Terry came home from work heavy-hearted. If only he could keep the latest hospital news to himself! No use trying. If Patti didn't see through him, Dad would.

Patti did. The minute Shane asked the blessing she said, "You may as well tell us." Her lips set in a thin line.

Terry saw her brace herself for bad news. "Fine thing for a chaplain," he said glumly. "I reflect change like a weather-vane in a hurricane."

"What happened?" she demanded.

"Mike reported another person refused to be brought to the hospital."

"What else?" Her clear gaze pinned him down.

"Isn't that enough?"

The relentless head shake brought a sigh and Terry cleared his throat. "Lindsey had a bit of trouble in surgery late last night."

"Trouble! How?" Her eyes resembled twin mountain lakes reflecting a cloudless sky.

"It happened during an operation. An important instrument turned up missing. Thank God the surgeon could substitute another instrument. The patient came through fine."

"Someone didn't set up properly?" Patti clutched the table with white-nailed fingers.

"That's the problem. Lindsey set up the table." Anger flared. Terry felt his blood boil at the blatant attempt to discredit the woman he loved. "She told me she personally checked, then double-checked the instruments shortly before surgery. I believe her."

"So do I!" Patti cried. "The rest of us make mistakes, but not Lindsey. Even when she's exhausted, she's never selected the wrong instrument or slipped up in any way." Crimson flags waved in her cheeks. "Terry, I'm going back."

"You can't! Don't you see? The viciousness of the attacks is increasing."

Patti paled but stood her ground. "I know. A patient might have died." She managed a wan smile. "I won't be sheltered any longer. These few days have given me time to get myself together. I'm going back to the hospital. If it takes pretending to go along with Bart Keppler, even getting engaged to him, I'll do it. I won't have Lindsey, you, and the hospital destroyed."

Terry expected a torrent of tears and marveled when they didn't come. He looked into the sweet face. His admiration grew. Here was a friend worthy of the name. Patti's set lips were the lips of a woman, not a much-admired girl.

"You not only can, you must," Shane said. "Finish your dinner. We'll miss you, but it's time for you to go back."

Before she and Terence drove away, the older man bade her kneel on the rug where she loved to curl up. He placed his hands on her head and asked God's protection, guidance, and wisdom for the difficult task that lay ahead. He closed by putting her in God's care. Terry had the feeling Patti would remember the blessing as long as she lived. So would he.

⟡

The days of Patti's absence had shown Lindsey a fuller view of her own heart when it came to Terence O'Shea. She knew he had spirited Patti away. She recognized the wisdom of no one knowing where. Yet a little ache came now and then despite her best efforts and Terry's plea, "Trust me, Lindsey." At last she admitted to a secret fear. The young chaplain's obvious admiration for her friend appeared to be growing like zucchini. Where did that leave Lindsey?

In vain she prayed, asking God to remove every hint of jealousy from her heart if Terry fell in love with Patti. She knew he spent every evening with the blonde nurse. Perhaps she had placed too much significance on the single kiss that now seemed an eternity ago. What did a kiss mean in the 1990s?

"It meant something to me," Lindsey confessed. She thought how all through the years she'd either been too busy or cared too little to date a great deal. Boys and men who attempted to turn evenings into a wrestling match found her unavailable for future dates. She just laughed and went her untroubled way when they called her old-fashioned and a prude.

All that changed when Dr. Keppler and Terence O'Shea came to the hospital. The attraction she had felt for the dark-haired acting director had been short-lived. Her feelings for the chaplain had not. Tired of fighting, she finally whispered into her pillow, "If this is how You want it, Lord, okay." The next second honesty forced her to add, "But I can't say I'll like it." She fell asleep smiling, less troubled than she'd been since Patti had been whisked away to some unknown destination.

The incident with the missing instrument shook her to the core. So did the unaccustomed reprimand from the surgeon in charge. She stood dumbly before him, unwilling to defend herself for fear of repercussions. Shina wanted to go to Nicholas Fairchild. Lindsey refused. He had enough to contend with just now without taking up the cause of a nurse who could prove nothing. Yet she couldn't help worrying.

"If this kind of thing keeps up, Terry and I will both be dismissed from Shepherd of Love for incompetence," she told Shina the day after the operating theater incident.

"It won't happen."

"It might and there isn't a thing I can do about it. If I say the table was sabotaged, every person in surgery will be questioned. I can't cast a slur on their integrity." She stared straight ahead, feeling caught on a treadmill that offered no escape.

A light tap sounded. The unlocked door swung open. Lindsey normally locked it only when she was out of the room but at Shina's insistence, she'd started bolting it except when Shina visited.

A blonde-haloed face peered in. "Looks like I've not even been missed."

"Patti!" Lindsey sprang from the couch and hugged the perky nurse. "You look wonderful."

"Why shouldn't I?" She blew a wispy curl off her forehead. "I've been milk, egg, and chicken fed. I've slept with the night breeze coming in my window—under an electric blanket, of course," she hastily added.

A rich chuckle came from the doorway.

Lindsey whirled. "She's been at the farm!"

"Yes, and a right good farm wife she'll make some lucky man." Terry's smiling face radiated affection.

Lindsey's heart dropped to the soles of her feet.

Patti laughed joyously. "Talk about blarney. Terence, take my suitcase to my temporary abode." She looked around the charming green apartment. "I can't wait to get back."

Terry's merry whistle and excellent spirits depressed Lindsey even more. Try as she would, she just couldn't be glad for Patti.

The smaller nurse flopped into a chair. "Good to be home, even though the farm is wonderful. I could fall in love with Shane O'Shea if I were older or he were younger."

"There's always his son." Lindsey managed to say.

"Are you kidding? You don't fall in love with a guy who's so gone on another woman he tells you so pointblank." Mischief lurked in Patti's eyes. "When are you going to give him a break, Lindsey? By the way, if you ever let on I said anything, I'll—I'll—I know," she cried. "I'll refuse to be in your wedding and it won't be legal." She spun around the room like a happy top.

"Only you could come up with something like that," Shina said cuttingly.

"I know. I'm awful." She looked repentant. "It's just that I missed you."

"Why did you come back?" Shina wanted to know. "If anything, things are worse, not better." She glanced at Lindsey.

Patti's impromptu dance broke off mid-step. "That's why." A deep flush stained her smooth cheeks. "Think I'm going to hide out on the farm and let my best friends in the whole world face this horror alone? A week ago, maybe. Not now. I'll have you know I'm going to take on Bart Keppler single-handed, if necessary."

"She looks like she means it," Shina said.

"I think she does." Lindsey felt the world slide from her shoulders and a light go on in her heart. If Terry cared enough to confide in Patti. . . She couldn't finish the sentence. When he came back, she saw the steady look he gave her. Unless she were completely off track, the sparkle of love lurked in his blue, blue eyes.

"So what's been happening?" Patti wanted to know. "I wormed a few things out of Terry but he's tighter than a clam when it comes to telling things. Well, sometimes," she tacked on.

Lindsey saw the black look he shot in Patti's direction. Delight filled her and a sense of well-being. Patti might exaggerate but even her over-active imagination couldn't conjure up a story unless enough truth existed to serve as a foundation.

"Black Bart asked me out again," Shina put in. "I said I'd go." The corners of her mouth turned down. "You know how crazy I am about that." She brightened. "Now that Patti's back, maybe he'll renege."

"One thing. I'm going to make the most of this opportunity. I do not intend to go out with T. D. M. more than once," Shina declared.

Patti yawned ostentatiously. "All the country air and relaxation left me beat. It's bed for me."

"Same here." Shina gritted her teeth. "A girl should look her best on every date—even if she can't stand her escort." She followed Patti into the hall, closing the door behind her.

"I feel as if a typhoon swept through here." Lindsey motioned Terry to a chair.

"Patti has that effect," he agreed. Lights danced in his eyes. "Did she say anything, uh, special, while I was out of the room?"

Lindsey couldn't have kept from blushing if her life depended on it. "Well—"

"It's all right," Terry told her. "I wanted to give you more time, but. . ." He stopped and she had the feeling he fought a battle. If so, he lost. In a swift movement, he caught her in his arms. "I know this isn't romantic and it's not at all as I planned, but hang it all, Lindsey, I don't know when we'll have time alone again. This whole hospital thing is messing up everyone and everything. I probably shouldn't be telling you this. We don't know what lies ahead." Poignancy softened his gaze. "I love you. I have since we collided in the dining room doorway. Right now all I have to offer you is that and what may be the worse part of 'for better or worse.'"

She placed one hand over his hips. "As if that matters."

"You mean it?" Worry lines smoothed out and Terry regained the boyish charm eclipsed by trouble in the past few weeks. He gently cupped her face in his hands.

"I do."

He pulled her hand free with one of his own, lowered his head until his lips touched hers and kissed her in a way guaranteed to send doubt packing and happiness surging through her.

Later, they sat side by side on the couch, Lindey's auburn head cradled against Terry's broad shoulder. She sensed a hesitancy, a certain withdrawal but could not identify it until he tentatively said, "About Dad—"

"He will be with us," she interrupted.

"Are you sure?" He held her away fro him so he could

look deep into her eyes. "Most brides don't want an in-law around, at least at first. We could make other arrangements. That is, if I still have a job."

She temporarily ignored the last sentence. "I'm not any bride and Shane O'Shea's certainly not any in-law. What better arrangement than for him to be with us?" She nestled closer to him. "Once we're married, I'll tell the powers that be: no more shift or nightwork. We'll come and go home together—to Dad."

"What did I ever do to have God give me such a wonderful companion?" Terry whispered.

She laughed, a tender, understanding laugh that showed the height and depth of a love that surpassed all but the love of God. "Funny. I was just thinking the same thing."

fifteen

A niggling worry about Shina accompanied Lindsey like a minor strain during her entire shift. Could the small nurse handle Dr. Keppler, if the need arose? Had they been wrong to encourage her to go out with him, even on a fishing-for-clues expedition?

Don't get paranoid, she told herself. *Bart wouldn't dare step out of line at this point. He's more apt to be charming and try to make a good impression. Wonder if Shina will learn anything? I can hardly wait to see her. Something has to break soon.* She sent up a quick prayer and went on with her work, grinning at the secret code the three nurses had set up. If Shina got home before Lindsey finished her shift, she'd slip a small piece of paper under Lindsey's door.

"What about me?" Patty had demanded, round blue eyes indignant.

"You'll hear me come in," Shina had reminded her. "Just make sure Black Bart drives away in his sports chariot before you come roaring down the hall to my room."

"Sports chariot! You're getting as fanciful with words as Lindsey."

"Who says you can't teach old dogs new tricks?" Shina had smirked. Her shining dark eyes showed her joy that the three of them were together and back on their old footing.

When her shift ended, Lindsey bundled up in the warm coat she'd taken the precaution to throw over her arm before going on duty. The afternoon had been sunny, but now the night was cold. Fresh, slightly salty air blew in from Puget Sound, snatching reluctant leaves from nearly bare branches and ruthlessly whirling them to the ground. Thanksgiving came late enough this year that they might get a skiff of snow. Despite the darkness around her, she brightened at the thought of the upcoming holiday. The entire Best family would be together, along with Terence O'Shea and his father.

Lindsey stepped into the covered passageway and gave a skip of pure happiness. Even the shroud of intrigue surrounding the hospital couldn't smother this precious time of loving and being loved.

She walked into the common gathering room of the residence hall and yawned. Bed certainly sounded good tonight. A slight stir in the dimly lit room set her heart shivering in her throat. "Who—?"

"Bart." His mouth smiled. His cold dark eyes did not. "I never get to talk with you, Lindsey. Is it true you're going to marry O'Shea?"

The last thing she wanted was a confrontation in a deserted room at this time of night. Summoning her most freezing tones she told him, "I can't see how that concerns you."

His hands shot out, gripping her arms above the elbow. "More than you know." An unpleasant smile turned his normally charming face into an ugly devil's mask. "I've been asked to stay on as hospital director, at least until next summer. Seems my predecessor needs extra time to recuperate." He casually added, "In the event something— unexpected—happens, I will be here permanently, with the power to hire and fire."

She tore free from his restraining hands. "Are you threatening me?"

"Let's just say if you value your position here, you'll be more tolerant of others' beliefs. I intend to make sweeping changes."

"The board of directors and Nicholas Fairchild will never permit that."

"Boards of directors, even hospital founders, can be replaced." The light of fanaticism in Dr. Keppler's dark eyes showed him to be dangerously close to the line between sanity and madness.

Lindsey's gasp acted like cold water in his face. In a chameleonlike shift, he again became the urbane doctor. "I hope I didn't frighten you, my dear." He laughed lightly. "I'm just so eager to do what's best for Shepherd of Love, to modernize it and make the hospital an example to the world, I sometimes get ahead of myself." His smile was full of charm. "Seriously, Lindsey, why can't we work together, rather than being at cross-purposes?" His expression grew tolerant. "You've even turned Shina against me. She refused a simple good-night kiss. Said she never kissed a first date."

"That's between Miss Ito and you, Dr. Keppler." Lindsey detoured around him, unlocked the door to the long corridor leading to her apartment, and stepped through. He started to follow. She forced a smile. "Sorry. I need to lock this behind me."

He held the door open and lowered his voice. "I was a fool to ever date Patti and turn you against me," he said. "Can't we go back to our first date? We were real friends then. I just tried to make you jealous. You're the woman I want for my wife. Can you forgive me?" His wistful penitence would have done credit to a martyr.

"Good night, Dr. Keppler."

He reluctantly released his hold on the door closing between them. "Good night, my darling."

The solid click of the lock had never been more welcome. Lindsey went limp against it for a moment before slowly walking down the hall. No need to check for Shina's piece of paper under her door. Her friend was safely in. Lindsey sighed with relief and tapped lightly.

Patti yanked the door open, blonde hair ruffled above a turquoise robe. "Hurry in," she whispered. "Just wait until you hear. Bart brought Shina home, hurried around to my door, and asked me to marry him! Can you believe it?" She made a horrible face. "I remembered my new role just in time and said I'd think about it, instead of slamming the door in his conceited face."

"You, too?" Lindsey felt a paroxysm of laughter well up inside her. She dropped to a chair. "He must plan to be a bigamist. He just proposed to me."

"How come I got left out?" Shina demanded, arms tucked into the flowing sleeves of the colorful kimono she wore in her room. "All he told me was since I didn't kiss guys good night on the first date, we must be sure to have another date as soon as possible."

They laughed until healing tears poured. Mopping her face, Lindsey sobered. "He's showing symptoms of insanity." She repeated their extraordinary conversation. "Something in his voice when he talked about Nicholas and the board of directors being replaced terrified me." She caught her breath. "That could explain the death threat Nicholas received. We can't wait any longer. I'm going to Terry tomorrow. He has to tell someone what's going on."

"Who?" Patti wanted to know. "If there's really a conspiracy, the hospital could be crawling with sympathizers to whatever cause Bart's supporting."

Lindsey felt herself blanch.

"She's right," Shina said. "The only person we can totally trust is Nicholas Fairchild himself."

≈

At eleven o'clock the next morning, Lindsey and Terence sat facing the man God had given the vision for Shepherd of Love. Item by item they poured out every happening, significant or otherwise, then repeated snatches of conversation that pointed toward Bart Keppler's duplicity.

"I knew beyond a shadow of a doubt when he used the Haitian word *combite*," Terry explained to the listening man whose eyes were shadowed with pain at the thought of evil in his beloved hospital. "He quickly added it must be neat to *combine* fun and farm duties, but I knew he'd lied earlier when he said he'd never been in Haiti."

They omitted nothing, even though Lindsey squirmed

when she reported Bart's proposals, first to Patti, then to herself. "I honestly think he's almost over the edge," she added. "Voodoo dolls are one thing. Frightening patients and stealing instruments laid out for surgery is something else."

"I agree." Nicholas clapped his hands together in a decisive gesture. "First, let me say I know you're incapable of criminal carelessness in your work, Lindsey. I have full confidence in you." He turned to Terence and smiled warmly. "And in you. Each of you represents the highest ideals of Shepherd of Love."

Lindsey held her eyelids wide open to keep back tears of gratitude.

"You're right about the situation worsening." Nicholas reached into his shirt pocket and withdrew a newspaper clipping. "This came shortly before you did." He read aloud:

> BIZARRE HAPPENINGS AT SHEPHERD OF LOVE?
> According to Dr. Bartholomew Keppler, acting director, reports of unusual incidents at the highly respected Seattle hospital are grossly exaggerated. "Nightmares can easily be construed as reality," Dr. Keppler says. "As far as the presence of voodoo dolls, I have seen no such evidence. Shepherd of Love will continue to serve the community as it has since its inception. I am personally spearheading a complete investigation but expect to find nothing."
>
> Dr. Keppler will continue at the helm of the hospital until the former director is fully recuperated and able to resume his duties.

"Clever move," Terry observed. "He comes off as a good guy while informing the entire city of Seattle something weird is going on at Shepherd of Love."

"How can anyone be so vile?" Lindsey burst out.

"I strongly suspect Dr. Keppler sincerely believes in what he's doing," Nicholas told them. His blue eyes shadowed. "I also suspect he's part of a satanic cult determined to infiltrate any institution dedicated to doing the Lord's work. I've known the time would come. Satan will not permit those who serve God to succeed, if he can possibly stop them. The important thing is, how are we going to stop him? If I tip off the board of directors and ask them to fire him, it also alerts Keppler's allies. There may be one on the board itself."

Terry thoughtfully fitted the fingertips of his hands together. "Right. You know the best way to catch thieves is to set another thief after them? I have an idea." He proceeded to outline it.

"It's too dangerous," Lindsey protested. "If it doesn't work. . ." The rest of the sentence rattled in her throat.

"It has to work." Terry ground his teeth and his eyes changed to November gray. "Don't forget. We'll have the element of surprise." He hesitated. "It's going to be hard on Patti. Can she do it?"

"She will have to. Besides, she's grown up a lot recently," Lindsey said.

Nicholas Fairchild had the last word. "Terence, tell only those who absolutely must know. We can't be sure how many have been snared into this thing." He rose, shook hands warmly, and told them to keep him informed.

Terry agreed to talk with Patti when she got off work; Lindsey would be on duty.

"She readily agreed," he told Lindsey over coffee in a deserted staff lounge during her break. He'd done some visiting and ended up outside Surgery on the chance he might see her. "When Bart presses her for an answer about marrying him, she's going to say, 'If you really love me,' then let her voice trail off. No promises, but he'll be self-centered enough to feel she accepted him. It should allay suspicion. That's phase one of Operation Hospital Rescue."

"Phase two concerns me more."

"I know." He stood, pulled her up, and let her head rest on his shoulder. "Don't worry, Lindsey. God is going to see us through. He actually has more at stake than we do. He won't allow evil to overcome work dedicated to Him."

Lindsey clung to him, raised her face for his kiss, then reluctantly freed herself. "Back to work for me." She added in a whisper, "When are you—?"

"Shhh." He placed a hand over her mouth. "You need to be surprised. A lot of our success depends on how well you play your part."

"Some comfort," she flared, then followed up with a grin. He left her at the door with a bland comment concerning how nice a quiet night in Surgery must be and headed down the hall without looking back. Lindsey wished he'd turn at the junction of the corridors, perhaps give her a thumbs-up signal. He didn't. She sighed, realizing they couldn't be sure no prying eyes watched.

☙

Dr. Keppler announced his engagement to Patti Thompson at breakfast the next morning. Lindsey tore her gaze from her friend's uncommunicative face and saw the malicious flash in Bart's eyes. She parried and thrust, choosing her words carefully. "Well, if congratulations are in order, they certainly should be given." She almost came unglued when Shina dropped her napkin on the floor, evidently to hide her feelings at the ambiguous, meaningless sentence.

Engrossed with his own importance, Bart didn't seem to notice. "We'll be married at Christmas." He attacked his eggs with gusto. "Have to postpone our honeymoon for a time, but that's okay with you, isn't it, Patti?"

"I don't care a thing about a honeymoon right now," she obediently agreed. A flash of humor twinkled in her eyes but by the time Bart looked up, Patti's long lashes rested on her flushed cheeks like little half-moons.

The door to the dining room opened. Nicholas Fairchild stepped inside. Something in his manner stilled table conversation. "I am sorry to interrupt your breakfasts," he quietly said. "Something has happened you need to know. Chaplain Terence O'Shea's father was admitted at six o'clock this morning."

"Shane?" "Oh, no!" Dismayed expressions came from every corner of the shocked room. Even those who hadn't met Shane knew how close Terry O'Shea was to his father. Lindsey felt sweat start on her forehead. Her heart twisted in sympathy for Patti, who looked as if she'd been hit.

Dr. Keppler sprang to his feet, face mud colored. "Will he be all right?"

"We certainly hope so. O'Shea will receive the attention he needs . Fortunately, we had a private room vacant on the second floor so he won't be disturbed." Nicholas strode out, leaving a buzz behind him.

Bart sat back down, face gray. Again Lindsey marveled. Keppler hated Terry. Why, then, did he look so stricken because the young chaplain's father now lay ill in Shepherd of Love? Not sure she could play out her part in the drama begun with Nicholas's announcement, Lindsey excused herself from the others and beat a retreat. She made sure no one was paying any particular attention to her, took a circuitous route, and ended up in the Chapel.

"So far, so good," Terry whispered into her ear once she got inside his study-office. He kept his lips close to her ear. "Dad's having the time of his life. Said he'd been feeling miffed at having to play silent partner in our sleuthing stunts. In addition, he's going to get his annual exam—by a doctor we've known for years. I had a little talk with Mallory, explained our plan, and got blasted." Terry laughed. "Once he came down from hitting the roof, he agreed to go along with it. Said something had to be done before human termites undermined Shepherd of Love internally and it collapsed around our heads."

"Do you think this will force Keppler to make his move?" Lindsey scarcely breathed, mindful of the bug Terry had found.

"No time like the present. Dad's all set up in his private room." Terry's grin didn't erase the anxiety in his eyes. "Says he feels like a piece of cheese in a rat trap. How did Nicholas do?"

"Great," Lindsey enthusiastically whispered. "He's almost as good with weasel words as I am. He appeared to say everything and really told nothing!"

Terry chuckled before longing filled his voice. "I just want this whole thing to end, so we can be together." He tilted her chin upwards and landed a kiss on her lips. "I have to go. Say a prayer."

"I will." She watched him go, shoulders squared against the upcoming ordeal. *God, grant a speedy end to this nightmare of evil.*

sixteen

Terence O'Shea fought drowsiness in the narrow confines of the small bath off the private room where his father lay peacefully sleeping. Anything that happened would be soon. Swing shift had long since given way to the influx of night workers. Now the hospital lay as silent as it ever became, the perfect time for enemy forces planning to strike. The bustle of Emergency, even Surgery, where angels of life and death observed no lull, felt far away.

Terry yawned and passionately wished for action. Better to get it over with, as he had told Lindsey. His lips curled in a smile. A warm glow filled him. During the long years of being too busy for love, of wondering if he would ever find the companionship Dad had shared with Mother, God had known the blessing that awaited him.

A slight scraping sound banished his pleasant thoughts. Terry noiselessly slid the bathroom door open a crack, enough to permit a full view of the dimly lit room. The partly raised window shade let in enough light for him to see anything that transpired. His heart skipped a beat when a dark, hooded figure inched through the door and crept toward the bed. It raised its arms. An almost inaudible mumbling began.

Terry felt cold sweat bead his forehead, even though he knew no supernatural being loomed over his father. His muscles tensed, preparing him to burst into the room and grapple with the figure. *Not yet*, an inner voice warned. He crouched, ready to spring, held back by his gut-level feeling.

One hand of the mysterious figure swept downward, disappeared into the capacious, enveloping black cloak, and withdrew an object. A voodoo doll? No. When held aloft, the object shone silver in the dim light.

Now!

Terry launched himself like a missile toward the hooded horror holding the hypodermic needle, tackled the figure around the waist, and seized the upheld arm.

For a moment the unexpected onslaught halted the murderous intruder. The hypodermic needle fell to the floor. Then with strength increased a hundredfold by fear, the figure writhed from Terry's grip, muttered a curse, and spun to face the young chaplain. Terry sucked in his breath. Instead of Dr. Keppler's face, a hideous painted mask stared at him.

A slight sound came from the bed. *Dear God, had Dad been harmed?* Terry whirled toward the bed, forgetting all else in a rush of terror.

The moment gave the intruder an advantage. It leaped for the doorway, pulled the door closed behind it.

"Go after him," Shane hissed.

"You're all right?"

"Fine. Now, go!"

Terry sprinted for the door, into the hallway. Not even a muffled footstep betrayed the presence of anyone foreign to the hospital. He hurried to the nearest nurses' station. "Did you see anyone pass this way?" he asked the LPN at the desk in a low voice, mindful of weary, sleeping patients who must not be disturbed.

"Why, no." She looked astonished. "This is the quietest night we've had in ages."

Terry hid his disappointment. "May I use the phone?"

"Of course. As long as you're here, I'll grab a cup of coffee."

The minute she got out of earshot, he dialed a number. "We've had an intruder. Follow anyone who leaves the hospital. Got it?" He hung up, chatted a moment with the returning LPN, and went back down the hall. His nerves twanged at the close call. No more playing bait for Dad.

Terry re-entered the private room, lighted now from the bed lamp Shane had switched on. He stared at his father.

Shane looked none the worse for the episode. He sat on the edge of his bed, one hand clutching something.

"What are you grinning about?" Terry demanded. "What if the backup plan fails? We won't have a shred of proof."

"Wrong." Shane's eyes gleamed with triumph. He slowly opened his clenched fingers and displayed a piece of paper. "Do you recognize these names?" he read them off.

Terry identified them as his father spoke. "Substitute ambulance driver. Surgery. Personnel. Maintenance. Member of the board of directors. Mostly women." Understanding came like a shaft of light. Was this why Bart dated every female employee at Shepherd of Love who would go out with him?

Excitement hoarsened his voice. "Dad, where did you get this?"

"I could say it was a gift from heaven. Actually, I found it on the floor when I turned on the light." His triumphant smile made him look more like Terry than ever. "Our night visitor dropped it in the scuffle. Wait until you hear what's on the back." He started reading. Every incident starting with the theft of the personnel records through the planned attack on Shane O'Shea had been documented. The single sheet of paper contained incontrovertible evidence to the existence of a conspiracy, enough to convict the writer beyond a shadow of a doubt. "Do you recognize the handwriting?"

"It has to be Keppler's." Terry sank to a chair. "Thank

God." He reached for the phone, got an outside line. "Detain suspect at all costs. Call me at this extension when you do." He somberly added, "Why would anyone keep such an incriminating piece of evidence?"

"Megalomania. Feelings of invincibility. Call it what you will. The obsessive need to have something to take out and gloat over will put Keppler—and others—away for a long time.

∂

The phone rang. Five times. Ten. Twenty. "Answer!" the caller pleaded, long black garment over one arm. Hollow suspicion grew into certainty. The unlisted number, to be used only in the direst emergency, was not going to be answered, for the man on the other end had fled. Who had tipped him off? What difference did it make? He'd obviously skipped, leaving the slaves who did the dirty work to face retribution.

He remembered terse instructions. "If it goes down, you're on your own. Expect no help. It would jeopardize future operations." Deadly emphasis came with the final order. "Don't get ideas about making a deal with the DA. You can't run fast enough or far enough to escape."

Had it been worth it, the skulking and toadying to one obviously inferior, the harassment and attempted murder? A fanatic light burned in a heart seized and made prisoner to the cause of Satan.

"Yes, a thousand times yes!" The hoarse cry echoed to the worn rafters of the miserable warehouse. "Tonight changes nothing. Let them run, the sniveling cowards. I will become the leader. No one suspects me."

Delusions of grandeur raised emotions to fever pitch. Filled with the desire to be possessed by the gods of darkness, the lone occupant of the abandoned warehouse slid into the black cloak. Black-garbed arms shot skyward. In-

cantations rose, whispered, but deadly as the figure went into a frenzied dance surely created by Satan.

A long time later, the spent worshiper considered the next move. "Must make contact." Fingers fumbled in the cloak, tore it off, shook it. Fear tasted metallic. It had to be there. Safety and the world's destiny depended on it! He seized the dark fabric, ripping it in his search.

❧

The warehouse door burst open. Beams of bright light caught and held the frantic figure like a fly in a spider's web. "Police. Freeze."

"Looking for something, Dr. Keppler?"

Bart started at the sound of his nemesis's voice. "O'Shea!" He tottered, regained his wits. "What is this? A belated Halloween joke?"

"No." An armed policewoman stepped forward. "What are you doing here?"

Some of his assurance returned. "I got a call saying if I wanted to learn who sent the death threats to Nicholas Fairchild, I should come here."

"Give it up, Keppler." Terry's slashing voice cut his excuse to ribbons. "A cloaked figure was followed by hospital security directly to this building. The cloak in your hands condemns you. So does this." He held up the list.

"You—" Bart hurled an epithet and lunged toward the chaplain. All the pent-up anger and frustration that had built each time Terry bested him rose in a tidal wave of hatred.

"Enough of that." Two policemen sprang forward, pinned Keppler's arms behind him, and handcuffed him.

The policewoman raised her voice. "Bart Keppler, I am placing you under arrest on suspicion of the attempted murder of Shane O'Shea. You have the right to remain silent. Anything you say can be used against you." She finished reading his rights. "Do you understand?"

He cursed, glared at Terry, and lurched toward the closely guarded door.

"The force is picking up the others," the policewoman said.

Bart's laughter rose, magnified by the desolate room. "You won't get the leader. He's long gone." Fanaticism gleamed in his dark eyes. "That God of yours may have won this time. Who cares? Our people are in every walk of life. Government. Hospitals. Churches. There's nothing you can do about it."

"No," Terry agreed. "But God can. Just as He did this time."

The laughter died, leaving silence more eerie than ever.

ਠਕ

Bart's prediction proved true. The roundup of those involved in the conspiracy failed to catch the Dr. Jekyll-Mr. Hyde board member who preserved the image of righteousness while working for the hospital's downfall. A search of his home turned up the full extent of the diabolical plan. Once Shepherd of Love's credibility vanished, personnel who refused to accept orders from Keppler were to be discredited and dismissed, replaced by those involved in devil worship.

The Seattle newspapers bloomed with headlines: GOOD TRIUMPHS OVER EVIL. ACTING HOSPITAL DIRECTOR CHARGED WITH ATTEMPTED MURDER. STRYCHNINE-FILLED SYRINGE DISCOVERED. SATANIC RITES NO MATCH FOR SHEPHERD OF LOVE. However, a few days later, attention shifted to a sensational robbery and the hospital returned to normal.

Thanksgiving morning, Lindsey rose, donned warm clothing, and stepped into a glistening world. An inch of white blanketed trees and lawns. A blue jay scolded from a snow-clad branch. A gray squirrel ran across the parking lot, leaving tiny tracks in the whiteness. Her heart swelled, as it did each time she saw a season's first, undisturbed snow.

Soon Terry and his father would arrive to take her to her parents' home for a day filled with laughter, love, promise. Now Lindsey cherished her time alone. She slowly walked to the exact spot where months earlier she had seen portentous black clouds hovering above the hospital. How much had happened since that long-ago day. A spark of evil had kindled, raged, been stamped out. A spark of friendship had kindled between her and Terry, deepened into love, and become an enduring flame.

She tilted her head back until the winter sun shone full on her face and turned in a circle. Mount Rainier, south and east, stood no more majestic than the Olympic Range across Puget Sound. A few stubborn clouds lingered in the blue sky, reminders that other storms would come. Lindsey shivered. In spite of the purity of the freshly painted world, at this very moment those who chose wickedness plotted to destroy right, beauty, holiness.

The clouds above Shepherd of Love moved on, driven by a brisk wind sweeping the sky like a magic broom. "Oh, God, help me treasure this day," she murmured. "And help me be strong for all the tomorrows."

"Amen to that." Two strong arms circled her. A husky voice asked, "Ready, dearest?"

Lindsey sent a final glance toward the hospital she loved. "Ready." With God beside them, she and Terence O'Shea could face whatever those unknown tomorrows might bring.

Coming soon from Heartsong Presents:

Shepherd of Love Hospital/Book Four:
Glowing Embers
by Colleen L. Reece

RN Nancy Galbraith and Dr. Damon Barton (originally appearing in *Flickering Flames*) know complete joy on their wedding day. Yet only God can give them strength to stamp out the glowing embers of hatred that threaten to destroy their marriage and perhaps their lives.

A Letter To Our Readers

Dear Reader:

In order that we might better contribute to your reading enjoyment, we would appreciate your taking a few minutes to respond to the following questions. When completed, please return to the following:

Rebecca Germany, Managing Editor
Heartsong Presents
P.O. Box 719
Uhrichsville, Ohio 44683

1. Did you enjoy reading *A Kindled Spark*?
   ❑ Very much. I would like to see more books
      by this author!
   ❑ Moderately
      I would have enjoyed it more if _____

   _____

2. Are you a member of **Heartsong Presents**? ❑Yes ❑No
   If no, where did you purchase this book? _____

   _____

3. What influenced your decision to purchase this
   book? (Check those that apply.)

   ❑ Cover   ❑ Back cover copy

   ❑ Title   ❑ Friends

   ❑ Publicity   ❑ Other_____

4. How would you rate, on a scale from 1 (poor) to 5
   (superior), the cover design? _____

5. On a scale from 1 (poor) to 10 (superior), please rate the following elements.

    ___Heroine   ___Plot

    ___Hero   ___Inspirational theme

    ___Setting   ___Secondary characters

6. What settings would you like to see covered in **Heartsong Presents** books?_____

_____

_____

7. What are some inspirational themes you would like to see treated in future books?_____

_____

_____

8. Would you be interested in reading other **Heartsong Presents** titles?   ❏ Yes   ❏ No

9. Please check your age range:
   ❏ Under 18   ❏ 18-24   ❏ 25-34
   ❏ 35-45   ❏ 46-55   ❏ Over 55

10. How many hours per week do you read? _____

Name _____

Occupation _____

Address _____

City_____ State_____ Zip _____

APPLES
FOR A
TEACHER

LESSON PLANS FOR LIFE

COLLEEN L. REECE
ANITA CORRINE DONIHUE

Apples for A Teacher is a bushel of short stories, poems, and prayers meant to delight and encourage teachers from any classroom. Offering a refreshing perspective on this profession, these apples are little ways that all say "Thank you for being my teacher." A perfect gift book that will be treasured by special teachers everywhere! 64 pages, Hardbound, 5" x 6 ½"

Send to: Heartsong Presents Reader's Service
P.O. Box 719
Uhrichsville, Ohio 44683

Please send me _____ copies of *Apples for A Teacher*. I am enclosing **$5.97 each** (please add $1.00 to cover postage and handling per order. OH add 6.25% tax. NJ add 6% tax.). Send check or money order, no cash or C.O.D.s, please. **To place a credit card order, call 1-800-847-8270.**

NAME _____

ADDRESS _____

CITY/STATE _____ ZIP _____

·····Hearts♥ng·····

CONTEMPORARY ROMANCE IS CHEAPER BY THE DOZEN!

Any 12 *Heartsong Presents* titles for only $26.95 **

Buy any assortment of twelve *Heartsong Presents* titles and save 25% off of the already discounted price of $2.95 each!

**plus $1.00 shipping and handling per order and sales tax where applicable.

HEARTSONG PRESENTS TITLES AVAILABLE NOW:

__HP 37 DRUMS OF SHELOMOH, *Yvonne Lehman*
__HP 38 A PLACE TO CALL HOME, *Eileen M. Berger*
__HP 41 FIELDS OF SWEET CONTENT, *Norma Jean Lutz*
__HP 49 YESTERDAY'S TOMORROWS, *Linda Herring*
__HP 50 DANCE IN THE DISTANCE, *Kjersti Hoff Baez*
__HP 53 MIDNIGHT MUSIC, *Janelle Burnham*
__HP 54 HOME TO HER HEART, *Lena Nelson Dooley*
__HP 57 LOVE'S SILKEN MELODY, *Norma Jean Lutz*
__HP 58 FREE TO LOVE, *Doris English*
__HP 61 PICTURE PERFECT, *Susan Kirby*
__HP 62 A REAL AND PRECIOUS THING, *Brenda Bancroft*
__HP 66 AUTUMN LOVE, *Ann Bell*
__HP 69 BETWEEN LOVE AND LOYALTY, *Susannah Hayden*
__HP 70 A NEW SONG, *Kathleen Yapp*
__HP 73 MIDSUMMER'S DREAM, *Rena Eastman*
__HP 81 BETTER THAN FRIENDS, *Sally Laity*
__HP 82 SOUTHERN GENTLEMEN, *Yvonne Lehman*
__HP 85 LAMP IN DARKNESS, *Connie Loraine*
__HP 86 POCKETFUL OF LOVE, *Loree Lough*
__HP 89 CONTAGIOUS LOVE, *Ann Bell*
__HP 90 CATER TO A WHIM, *Norma Jean Lutz*
__HP 93 IDITAROD DREAM, *Janelle Jamison*
__HP 94 TO BE STRONG, *Carolyn R. Scheidies*
__HP 97 A MATCH MADE IN HEAVEN, *Kathleen Yapp*
__HP 98 BEAUTY FOR ASHES, *Becky Melby and Cathy Wienke*
__HP101 DAMAGED DREAMS, *Mary Hawkins*
__HP102 IF GIVEN A CHOICE, *Tracie J. Peterson*
__HP105 CIRCLE OF LOVE, *Alma Blair*
__HP106 RAGDOLL, *Kelly R. Stevens*
__HP109 INSPIRED LOVE, *Ann Bell*
__HP110 CALLIE'S MOUNTAIN, *Veda Boyd Jones*
__HP113 BETWEEN THE MEMORY AND THE MOMENT, *Susannah Hayden*
__HP114 THE QUIET HEART, *Rae Simons*
__HP117 FARTHER ALONG THE ROAD, *Susannah Hayden*
__HP118 FLICKERING FLAMES, *Connie Loraine*
__HP121 THE WINNING HEART, *Norma Jean Lutz*
__HP122 THERE'S ALWAYS TOMORROW, *Brenda Bancroft*
__HP125 LOVE'S TENDER GIFT, *Elizabeth Murphy*
__HP126 MOUNTAIN MAN, *Yvonne Lehman*

(If ordering from this page, please remember to include it with the order form.)

········ **Presents** ········

Great Inspirational Romance at a Great Price!

Heartsong Presents books are inspirational romances in contemporary and historical settings, designed to give you an enjoyable, spirit-lifting reading experience. You can choose wonderfully written titles from some of today's best authors like Veda Boyd Jones, Yvonne Lehman, Tracie J. Peterson, Nancy N. Rue, and many others.

When ordering quantities less than twelve, above titles are $2.95 each.

SEND TO: Heartsong Presents Reader's Service
         P.O. Box 719, Uhrichsville, Ohio 44683

Please send me the items checked above. I am enclosing $_____
(please add $1.00 to cover postage per order. OH add 6.25% tax. NJ
add 6%.). Send check or money order, no cash or C.O.D.s, please.
         To place a credit card order, call 1-800-847-8270.

NAME _____

ADDRESS _____

CITY/STATE_____ ZIP _____

                                        HPS 10-96

Heart♥ng Presents
Love Stories Are Rated G!

That's for godly, gratifying, and of course, great! If you love a thrilling love story, but don't appreciate the sordidness of some popular paperback romances, **Heartsong Presents** is for you. In fact, **Heartsong Presents** is the *only inspirational romance book club*, the only one featuring love stories where Christian faith is the primary ingredient in a marriage relationship.

Sign up today to receive your first set of four, never before published Christian romances. Send no money now; you will receive a bill with the first shipment. You may cancel at any time without obligation, and if you aren't completely satisfied with any selection, you may return the books for an immediate refund!

Imagine. . .four new romances every four weeks—two historical, two contemporary—with men and women like you who long to meet the one God has chosen as the love of their lives. . .all for the low price of $9.97 postpaid.

To join, simply complete the coupon below and mail to the address provided. **Heartsong Presents** romances are rated G for another reason: They'll arrive *Godspeed!*

YES! Sign me up for Heart♥ng!

NEW MEMBERSHIPS WILL BE SHIPPED IMMEDIATELY!
Send no money now. We'll bill you only $9.97 post-paid with your first shipment of four books. Or for faster action, call toll free 1-800-847-8270.

NAME _____

ADDRESS _____

CITY _____ STATE _____ ZIP _____

MAIL TO: HEARTSONG PRESENTS, P.O. Box 719, Uhrichsville, Ohio 44683

YES10-96